VIVID

by ANDREA MURRAY

DMP

Dragon Moon Press

Cover Design by Greg Simanson

This book is a work of fiction. The names, characters, places, and incidents are imaginary and fictitious. Any resemblance to persons (living or deceased), true events, real locations or organizations is coincidental.

Print ISBN 978-1-988256-08-5
EPUB ISBN 978-1-988256-09-2

Library of Congress Control Number: 2014918333

This book is dedicated to Terry whose life and death showed us all how precious our time on this planet really is. We miss you, Big 'T'.

PROLOGUE

WHEN I WAS FIVE, I watched my mother die.

My memories aren't crystal clear, more like looking through a fogged-up window. I don't remember why we were standing near a river or why she was smiling and holding my hand.

I do remember the stormy sky, the strobe lightning, and the screaming—always the screaming.

CHAPTER ONE

"DAMN, DAMN, DAMN!" I fumble with my lock. This is my fourth lock of the year—a new record—and all the combinations and number patterns from the previous fatalities keep pushing their way to the front of my mind. I smack my hand against the front of my locker as though it's responsible for the jerks who keep forcing me to buy new locks.

In this high school if you aren't one of 'them' then apparently you deserve whatever punishment 'they' feel is necessary to weed you from the pack. Call it a survival of the fittest check-up.

In my case someone keeps stealing my combination or just cutting my lock but that only happened to lock number two, probably because it required a key, not a stolen combo. I always try to remember to roll the dial on the lock or shield my hand when I put in the combination, but someone is way too interested in vandalizing my stuff.

I never understood that. If they hate me so much, why do they waste their time on me? I mean, it makes no sense that someone they see as unworthy occupies so much forethought in their group conscience. (I firmly believe they must all share the same brain.)

I'm not their only victim. I'm just the only one who ever fights back, fights that typically aren't physical but are always a pain in the ass and somehow end with me in the principal's office while the flawless, plastic-people never seem to get caught, making me look like a 'troubled teen'.

It started in junior high when we all moved from the separate middle school campuses. The haves versus the have nots, the cool versus the losers, the populars versus all the rest of us who weren't blessed with perfect features, perfect bodies, and perfect lives. In the center lives the queen bee, Trista Parmer, blonde, tall, tan even in winter, and totally vicious. I've never figured out why she hates me, and at this point, I don't even care anymore. I simply want to stay out of her line of fire.

I've just put my forehead on the cool, blue metal locker, ready to give up, when my salvation arrives in the form of a plump, curly-haired blonde, pushing up her purple-rimmed glasses at the same time she pushes me away from the locker.

Abby Johnson has a way of making her 5-foot presence seem much larger. We've been best friends since this nightmare started in seventh grade when I helped her pick up her books after Trista knocked them out of her hands in front of half the school. We take care of each other. She memorizes my locker combos and gives me rides since I have yet to get a car even though I've had my license since I turned sixteen last April, and I, well, I'm not sure what I do for her unless you count insisting she stay at my house when her useless parents are away (and they are *always* away). I've lived with my Aunt Charlotte since I was five. She took me in when my mom was killed, and we've kind of adopted Abby, made her an honorary member of the family, not that that means much.

As Abby's fingers fly over my lock, I notice her new, expensive jeans with the rhinestone hearts swirled on the back pockets and her pink shirt that cost more than I spend in a month. She has one of the qualifications to be a 'them'. She has money. Her parents are loaded because her dad is some kind of investment broker, and her mom is a big shot executive. They travel sometimes as many as four days a week, but since the housekeeper found a bottle of tequila in Abby's room three weeks ago, they've made a "new commitment to Abby and the family," at least that's what her dad told her. So basically this means they're trying to stay home more and snarl at each other less.

They didn't even punish Ab for the alcohol she took from their own den. She thought if she showed up at the Valentine's Day lake party that Trista was throwing earlier this month she might finally be accepted by them, and they might leave her alone.

"Call it a peace offering," she had said as we drove out to the party in her car. I didn't bother to get out, hadn't even changed out of my ratty sweat pants and hoody. She was dressed in what she calls her 'skinny-girl' outfit of jeggings and a low-cut sweater. She wanted so much to make a good impression, the impression she thought they wanted to see. But the whole thing was an epic failure when she came back to the car, unopened bottle in hand. They'd all been wasted and laughed at her. I don't know why she wants to be accepted by that bunch of fakes, but that's just Abby I guess. She's not even close to being as tough as she wants to appear. All of this races through my mind as she opens the door and turns to me, lock in hand.

"Bad day?" Abby sighs.

"You have no idea." I run my hand through my long, reddish-brown hair. That's my nervous habit, and if this year doesn't end soon, I may end up bald.

"So spill. What happened this time? The dime squad?" That's what we call the popular girls, all those cookie-cutter '10s' – identical, disposable, and easily-tossed around. Ok, maybe not that last one, but a girl can dream.

Instead of answering, I hand her the rumpled paper I've been gripping in my left hand and tug on my t-shirt in frustration. She smoothes the paper enough to see the red writing on the top of the page.

"You are the only person I know who stresses over a 98%. It's not normal, Viv. Normal people WANT good grades. Let me guess" — she rolls her eyes — "highest in the class?"

When I just turn and stare at the back of my locker, she shakes her head, smiles, and lays her hand on my back.

"I don't get it, V. If I were like genius smart, I'd smear it in all of their faces! Don't give me that look, Vivian Cartwright. Why pull your punches? Why do you even bother to try at all if you won't let yourself make the grades you're capable of making? I know, I know. I've heard it before."

She stops and does the air quote thing which she knows drives me crazy and tries to make her voice sound like mine. "You 'don't want any attention,' at least not more than you already get."

"I am not that whiney, and it's not just the grade." I run my hand through my hair again. "It's the lock and the grade and the fact that this morning Mr. Thompson asked me to serve on prom committee," I say, ticking off each catastrophe and throwing my hands up in surrender.

Abby turns my shoulders, forcing me to face her and gasps, "Prom committee?!" Her blue eyes are wide, her expression unbelieving. "I thought prom committee had been chosen a long time ago. I mean, this is like the end of February; prom's in two months. Haven't they already been meeting? Do you have to? What are you going to do?" With each question, her eyes get bigger and bigger, and she seems to be holding her breath, waiting for my reply.

"Yes, no, and definitely not happening," I say in answer to her questions. "Apparently, Taylor Johnson can no longer serve because of some issue with grades, and Mr. Thompson thought it would be good for me, help me out of my shell." I roll my eyes at the stupid cliché. He's not the first teacher who has tried to help me, to save me from my future life as the lonely cat lady. Teachers think they have to make a somebody out of everybody. Don't get me wrong; Aunt Charlotte is a kindergarten teacher, so I know how hard they work and everything, but come on! Some of us just want to survive this hellhole and move on without their interference.

I feel the need to continue reassuring Ab if for no other reason than to return her eyes and breathing to normal. "You know I don't need any more hassle with Trista and her acolytes."

"Oh, thank God!" She releases her breath with a whoosh and grabs me in a bone-crushing hug, and I know she thinks I made the right choice. Prom committee would most definitely put me on the dime squad radar even more than I am already. She pulls away from me so quickly I might have tripped backward if she hadn't held on to my upper arms. I may be three inches taller than Abby (a whole 5'3", thank you very much), but she definitely can hold her own, as Aunt Charlotte says.

"Come on; let's go to lunch. I brought you a cupcake." She shakes her polka-dot lunch tote and talks to me like Aunt Charlotte used to when I was little and wouldn't eat my veggies. "The kind you like with the super-sweet icing."

She tugs my shirt as I grab my black, nylon lunch bag, slamming my locker with my free hand and not even bothering with the lock since I can't remember the combo anyway.

As we wind our way around the hall stragglers, I wonder how she does that, how she makes me feel better and seems to know what I need. As long as I have Abby, the dime squad, the jocks, the emos, all the cliques, can kiss my ass. Just a year and four months and I'll be gone, out of this town. I'll earn a great scholarship, and finally go somewhere new, somewhere better. I can do that. I can survive that. And I suddenly wonder just who I'm trying to convince.

CHAPTER TWO

AHH, THE CAFETERIA, probably my least favorite place on the planet. The place where I am forced to mingle with the gossiping masses but, more importantly, the place where Queen Trista and the dime squad reign supreme at the center table. I've tried hiding out at lunch, but I keep getting caught and sent back, a la *Groundhog's Day*, to relive the same crap as the day before.

I take it all in, the 1970s multi-colored chairs in putrid shades of green, orange, and brown; the mind-numbing noise level equivalent to a small jet engine; the nauseating smell of... I'm really not sure what that smell is (nor am I sure I want to)—maybe brown beans, ensuring all of the boys will be gassed up and making our afternoon classes less than pleasant.

The room is already pretty full when Abby and I enter through the side door, skipping the small line at the serving counter. The usual groups are already there in their spots. Trista is surrounded by her friends, all of them so alike they could be the same person. She glances my way, giving a lop-sided sneer. She's dressed like she should be going to some party with her skinny jeans and silky, low-cut top. Is she wearing stilettos? Who wears high heels to school? When she turns back, she says something that makes them all laugh hysterically. I'm sure she still thinks her recent prank on my locker is supremely clever.

We are peripherals, sitting on the edge of the herd. We like to sit at the farthest table in the back of the room, our backs to the wall with the big 'Home of the Bulldogs' painting, a cartoon dog complete with red t-shirt, disproportionately muscular arms, and a fierce scowl that seems to taunt all of us who don't fit in. If we sit there, we can scan the room and make fun of all of those people we aren't cool enough to be. It makes us feel empowered even if it's only for forty minutes every day.

I can't think about this too hard because then the rational part of my brain will realize how pathetic this little ritual truly is.

Today, I'm feeling particularly crabby, and I am so ready for a round of 'they're the real losers' with Abby when I notice our usual seats are taken. I follow Abby's lively step, watching her curls flop vigorously. She's babbling in her bubbly way about some new, cute boy she saw in the office this morning.

"I really hope he's a junior, too. Maybe we'll have classes together! He was so hot, V. You've got to see him. We'll look for him during lunch." She looks toward the front and stamps her foot, making her glasses slip slightly down her nose. "Oh crap! He's sitting with the dime squad. I swear if Trista gets her claws into him I'll—" but she never finishes her sentence because she sees the two girls sitting in our normal seats.

She stares open-mouthed at the invaders and stops so suddenly I almost bump into her.

"What the heck? Who is *that*, and why are they in *our* chairs?" She points at the girls as though I haven't already noticed them. I've seen the girls in the hall a few times, and I think I might have had study hall with the brunette back in eighth grade year. But I don't know their names.

Abby stomps her short frame over to our chairs, pulls back her shoulders, and puffs out her rather ample chest. With her frizzy, yellow hair, she looks like an angry cockatoo. I want to laugh as I trail behind her, but I know that would totally ruin the effect she's trying to achieve. Abby wants to think she's a bad ass, and a lot of people probably believe it, but I know better. It's the tough front, the hard shell she's built up to protect herself from her own feelings of worthlessness because her parents are never there for her, and her only friend is an outcast.

"Hey, these are our seats. Move." Abby glares over the top of her square glasses. She flicks her wrist like she's swatting a fly.

The two girls, whom I now remember seeing hanging on the fringe of the dime squad, just ignore Ab and continue their obviously fake conversation about something that happened in PE. They're making exaggerated hand gestures in an attempt to appear nonchalant, to make our presence seem completely unimportant.

"Yeah, so he said he only dated older girls, so I hit him with the volleyball, right in the nuts!" The blonde laughs snidely. The other girl, the brunette, just smiles nervously. She apparently isn't comfortable with something.

Abby's face has turned an angry pink by this point; her hands have found their way to her hips. Arms akimbo, she steps closer to the blonde sitting near the end of the table in what is normally Abby's chair. Her lunch bag dangles from her fist.

"Maybe you didn't understand me. Let me start again." She drops her lunch bag on the table. "These" — she points to the chairs — "are our" — points to the two of us — "seats" — points back to the seats again. "You" — points to them — "move." She makes a walking gesture with her fingers.

The girls, who've stopped talking during this little instructional session, are now glaring back at us. The blonde sticks her nose in the air. "I don't see your names on them." The classic elementary school response.

"Oh yeah? Maybe you should stand up, and I'll show you our names." This from Abby the Bitch Slayer. I can't contain myself anymore, and I finally let go with the snort of laughter I've been holding in since Abby's march across the cafeteria.

But then I notice how quiet the typically noisy room has grown, and I realize we've been set up. Someone has put these girls up to this stunt, and when I look around, I see Trista, homecoming princess, prom queen nominee, and total bitch, smiling back at me. In fact, the entire dime squad and most of their current arm-candy boyfriends are smiling, too. I also notice that another girl has moved behind me, blocking any escape route.

Two thoughts cross my mind: 1. Where the hell are the duty teachers? 2. Stay calm so no one gets hurt. When I get mad, really mad, bad things happen—abnormal, lock-you-away-and-experiment-on-you things. It's been this way since I was a little kid. It's one reason I try to stay away from them. Whatever they do to me is nothing compared to what I might accidentally do to them.

One of my most vivid memories happened around the time of my mom's death. I remember hearing my mom scream, and I remember being so angry I couldn't hear anything but her screaming. Then a huge tree near a flapping tent exploded into tiny slivers like tree confetti.

When I was nine, the boy down the road stole my bike, and when I saw him riding it the next day, he suddenly went flying backward off of the bike and crashed against the side of my house. We told everyone he'd hit a rock and lost control of the bike. Aunt Charlotte had agreed to pay to have his broken leg fixed and told me I had a 'gift' which I would have to learn to control. And I did. I learned to use my breathing to calm down—give myself little time outs every time I felt myself getting upset, and for four years, I was incident-free.

The last time I forgot to control myself was during the summer of seventh grade year. I went swimming at the local pool, and when I dove off of the highest diving board, my suit came untied on one of my shoulders. I was, of course, completely unaware of this catastrophe in the making, and when I surfaced so proud of myself for conquering my fear of the jump, my suit had slipped down on one side. Half of my pathetically small assets were exposed for all to see. I yanked it up as soon as I realized, praying no one witnessed my humiliation; unfortunately, Trista was there, and she pointed and laughed, making sure everyone who didn't see it happen at least knew about it. I was so mortified and angry that I climbed out of the pool and ran all the way home but not before I accidentally caused the windows in the two cars parked in front of the pool entrance to explode. Maybe that was the moment I became her target, an insecure baby who ran instead of standing up to her.

So, my thought about the teachers is just as much a fear for the safety of these girls—Trista's pawns—as it is for Abby and me. I've tried so hard to stay 'normal'. That's why I don't make the top grades, win top honors, because I don't want anyone to see me too closely. When I realized what I could do, it scared the hell out of me. And making things explode or fly through the air are only a couple of the talents I possess. There is a whole list of freaky things I can do. That's a huge responsibility. One bad thought, one slip of my control, and someone could be dead. It's a talent I wish I didn't possess.

Even Abby doesn't know any of this; no one except Aunt Charlotte knows.

I glance behind me at the girl stationed there, practically standing on top of me. She is massive with spiky hair and so many piercings that she's probably setting off metal detectors fifty miles away. She puts her hands on my shoulders, grounding me to the spot. This chick is definitely not dime squad material like the two girls in our seats. They may be doing this to join the in-crowd, but big mama is not, and I wonder why the dime squad has taken to hiring a hit man/girl.

Totally unaware of what is happening behind us, Abby just keeps running her mouth.

"I said get up!" I put my hand on Abby's upper arm because I know this is going to be more than a simple prank. *That* I'm not afraid of; I can handle the vandalized locker, the ugly names. I can even handle when they steal my clothes during PE. But *this*... this is going to be bad.

CHAPTER THREE

OKAY, I'M THINKING maybe I can defuse this thing and not appear like a total chicken, but when the blonde stands and pours her energy drink right over Abby's head, I know how wrong I am. I tighten my grip on Abby's arm at the same time she lunges for the girl, and total chaos ensues.

The blonde and her pal jump up and run around the table toward the safety of the dime squad. I yank Abby to my chest to keep her from following them while Goliath girl spins me and a damp, squirming Abby around to stare into her pin-cushion face. She leans right down into my face, less than an inch from actually touching her lip hoop to my forehead.

I feel her rancid breath on my face, and judging by the smell, she must have had the beans.

"Trista wants to make sure Two-Ton Thompson didn't talk you into prom committee."

"What? How do you..." Wow, news did travel fast around here. "No, you can tell your 'boss' that I'm not joining the committee." I can't believe I am saying this to monster girl without cowering under the table.

I also can't believe the nerve of Trista! What did she promise this behemoth to play her enforcer? I thought the dime squad was harmless, annoying, but harmless. Now, they seem a bigger threat. Could she have paid this girl to threaten me? Probably, since it's unlikely that Trista would be able to do anything for her. In this moment, I realize how far Trista and her crew will go to get what they want and just how far-reaching her control truly is. If she would stoop to physical violence, what else would she be willing to do?

"Good because I'd hate to waste any more of my lunch on messin' up your face." Then she pushes me, and since I still have a grip on Abby, we both fall hard on our butts right there in front of the entire school.

The cafeteria erupts into laughter. As I look around, I see a few non-laughing faces, mostly on those kids who probably suffer Trista's humor just like me and surprisingly on a few of the faces at the jock table. I can feel my anger building like lava being forced to the surface while I suffer the humiliation.

Got to calm down. I take a deep breath and close my eyes. Calm down. Deep breath. I try to think of peaceful images: a beach, a mountain stream, Trista's head on a spear—okay, that's not helpful, and this is not working. Then I hear Abby whimper and open my eyes to see her cradling her left wrist close to her chest.

"You okay?" I ask, trying not to see her chin tremble or the tears filling her eyes.

"My wrist." She squeezes the words out between lips she's trying to keep tightly closed so that she won't break down. "I must have fallen on it. I think it might be broken." Her eyes convey clearly what she's about to do.

"Don't you cry in front of them," I whisper.

"Ah is wittle Abby Wabby gonna cry?" Sasquatch girl rubs her fists over her eyes to mimic a baby. She bends down closer to Abby.

When Abby drops her head and a single tear splashes on her injured wrist, the volcano erupts. I feel a tingle in my feet and hands. The tingle moves quickly up my legs and arms. When it reaches my chest, the tingle becomes a burst. I squeeze my eyes closed again, this time as tightly as possible, trying to push the feeling back down because I know what's going to happen. I'm struggling, and I'm failing.

Behind my eyelids I actually see a tiny light like a dot at the end of a long tunnel. It grows, becoming larger and larger, and I envision a freight train speeding down a track. The light grows until it bursts like an exploding star.

I open my eyes, and everything looks different, like tunnel vision only around the edges there is bright, white light, and locking on my target, I realize I have lost control.

"Hey, look," our tormentor teases, rising and looking around at everyone. "She's so fat she probably broke her wrist by sitting on it! Little piggy, I think I might just smack you around for the hell of it!"

When she bends back down and grabs Abby's shoulder, I clinch her forearm. I feel my strength. I look down at my arm. My whole body is covered in goose bumps, and the tiny hairs on the back of my neck are standing up. If I were to look in a mirror right now, I know my eyes would be losing their usual gray color, becoming completely colorless around the black pupils, and glowing like a nightlight. This girl is a good seven or eight inches taller than me and has biceps a linebacker would envy, but at this moment, none of that matters.

Her look of amusement flashes to one of anger, then confusion. I release Abby and slowly stand, maintaining my hold on the girl. Gripping her arm hard, I push her back several steps. Just like a scene from one of those cheesy '80s high school movies, silence descends in a wave across the cafeteria.

But this girl doesn't realize yet that she should give up this fight she's about to lose. "You little bitch! I'm gonna—hey! What are you doin' to my arm?"

She wraps her free hand over my own since I'm still clutching her arm like a vise. Her whole body starts to shake, and she falls to her knees gripping my hand and trying to pry my fingers off. I can feel her jagged nails raking my hand and forearm, but I know nothing can break the contact until I choose to break it. My mind is screaming to let go while there is still time to salvage this situation, to keep anyone from seeing my eyes, to keep this girl from being seriously hurt, and to keep from appearing as anything other than a typical student in this school. But my body, my hand, refuse to listen.

"Stop! What are you doin' to me?" On her face is a look of both panic and pain. I maintain eye contact with her; I can't do otherwise. For these few seconds, we are totally connected. I can actually hear her thoughts and see into her mind, and she's afraid, very afraid. This girl has never been truly afraid until now. She is petrified, more of her failure to intimidate me than of the actual pain she is feeling. I can feel her fear in every cell of my body, and though it scares *me* to admit it, I think I like knowing she is scared of me. This is a power I haven't let myself experience in so long, and it feels exhilarating. There will be repercussions, but right now, I don't care!

I am standing between her and the majority of the gawking student body. I lean down into her face, just as she had done to me earlier, and force her arm to bend so that it is between my body and hers.

"Your eyes... what the hell are you?" Her arm is beginning to smoke slightly beneath my fingers, and I can smell burning hair. I jerk her right into my chest, as though she weighs nothing, crushing her arm and the smoking skin between us. I put my mouth close to her ear.

"Haven't you heard? I don't play well with others," I whisper, and my voice sounds strange, stretched tight like a rubber band. Finally, my brain takes control again, and I release her, pushing her away from me. She lands on her back and quickly sits up. She clasps her wrist to her chest, now in the same position as Abby.

The girl lets go of her wrist to assess her injury, and I see dark red marks shaped like my fingers, maybe even a blister or two around the edges. I look at my own hand where, in the center, a jagged line glows blue, snaking down my palm like lightning. I squeeze my hand and eyes closed, and when I look again, the mark is gone, my palm my own again. Then I turn to face the aftermath.

CHAPTER FOUR

THE MAN ACROSS FROM ME holds the fate of the remainder of my junior year in his hands. Mr. Sailers sighs heavily and looks at me as he takes off his glasses and tosses them atop the open file with my name emblazoned across the tab in his scrawling hand writing. He rubs his balding head and looks up at the ceiling.

"Vivian, you promised me on"—he pauses to glance down at what I assume is my ever-growing punishment record—"December 10th, that you would not be setting foot inside this office again this school year." He leans back in his leather chair and folds his hands across his stomach.

"I know, sir, but really it's not my fault." I try for a regretful tone, widening my eyes in my best imitation of a cartoon puppy dog. I try for the trembling lip without success.

"Not your fault! Betty Sanders left here with what appeared to be burns on her arm after you assaulted her in a cafeteria full of people!"

"The giant man-girl's name is Betty? Really?" I don't realize I've spoken this aloud until I see the shade of red that is Mr. S's face become even darker, and he sits up so quickly he nearly knocks over the cup of coffee sitting near the edge of his desk. I'm pretty sure his head is going to combust any second now.

"Sorry, sir. Look I'm really sorry about"—I nearly choke on the snicker bubbling up at saying the name—"Betty's arm, but really how could I have possibly done that? Yes, we argued, and yes, I grabbed her, but only after she pushed both Abby and me. It was self-defense all the way."

The part about being sorry is only partially true. I am sorry about her arm but only because people will ask questions I can't and won't answer. I don't give two shits about Big Betty's injury, but of course I can't tell him that.

It briefly enters my brain that I should try harder to cry. This offense might require I squeeze out a few tears to keep from getting a major punishment. So, I conjure up as many sad images as possible in a twenty-second time spam, but I just can't do it. I'm not sad about what I did. It feels pretty damn good, truth be told.

"I understand that," he continues while I'm still trying to muster up some moisture, "and Betty will also be punished when she returns, but right now we're discussing you, Vivian." He pauses and perches his glasses close to the end of his nose, tilting his head up to read through them.

"You have such an exemplary academic record. I just don't understand. Help me understand, Vivian." He sighs and taps on the page in front of him.

The way he keeps saying my name reminds me of how TV attorneys badger a witness, and I want so badly to say 'I object' or something legal-sounding like that. Instead I offer the only explanation possible. "Mr. Sailers, I am not a troublemaker. Trouble in the form of the dime sq—uh, I mean Trista Parmer and her friends, always finds me."

"Yes, I've heard all of this before—how these girls harass and bully you and how you and Abby Johnson are the victims, and I've told you to bring me proof." He pauses, sighs again and continues, "But you have yet to do so."

"They're sneaky, Mr. S! It's always he said/she said, no physical evidence to tie them to the harassment." Now who sounds like a lawyer?

"Well, the 'evidence' this time is very clear; while you maintain that Trista somehow bribed Betty to fight you, Betty says otherwise."

Betty the Behemoth had told Sailers I'd provoked her when she defended her 'friends' who were inadvertently sitting in our usual seats. Her friends? Right! All of that tattooed giant's friends are either on parole or in jail. I'm 100% sure she would rather kill and devour those girls sitting in our seats than befriend them.

"Ok." It's my turn to sigh. "I give up, Mr. S. What's it going to be this time? Detention? Sweeping the halls again? Or my personal favorite, a warning to 'never do this again or else'?" I'm really hoping for the last one, but I'm thinking that's probably not happening this time. I give him my sweet-girl smile and blink my eyes all innocent (curses, still no tears!), cross my hands in my lap, and pray those famous 'I will save this kid' teacher feelings kick in and make Mr. Sailers have mercy. Yeah, those same feelings I was bitchin' about earlier—those are the ones I need right now.

Mr. S gets up from his desk and walks toward the big window facing the parking lot. Uh oh, he's never done that before. He turns his back to me and stares out the window for a minute or so, just long enough to have me sweating and nervous. I stare at the back of his yellow dress shirt while he rubs his chin. My stomach suddenly doesn't feel so hot. He turns toward me.

"Vivian, normally I would suspend you three days for fighting, but in light of your outstanding grades, I have a better idea. We have some students in need of tutoring. All of these boys are athletes in jeopardy of losing eligibility. I thought I'd found tutors for all of them, but Coach Wilson informed me of a last-minute addition just this morning. You may choose. A three day suspension with zeroes in all your classwork for those three days or tutoring sessions until this boy's English average is a 'B' or better, however long that may take."

I inhale sharply and stare out the same window Mr. S had earlier. The bell is ringing, and I watch the kids trickle out to their cars. "So, let me make sure I understand. If I choose option B, I am this kid's tutor indefinitely?"

"No, just until his average is a 'B'."

"But that could take the rest of the year if he's a dumb ass! Sorry, sir, I mean if he's not motivated and giving his best effort."

He clears his throat and straightens his shoulders, and I'm really surprised when he doesn't yell at me for my bad language. He rubs his chin again in an effort to hide his smile. Guess it's kinda minor in comparison to almost igniting a girl, huh?

"Those are your choices, Miss Cartwright. Decide now."

Let's see... hmm... three days of zeroes would mean lower grades which could mean no chance at a scholarship next year and therefore no chance to escape this town. Or God knows how many after-school sessions with some stupid jock who barely knows the alphabet song and who will probably (correction, most definitely) make fun of me in front of his big shot jock friends and the dime squad since a lot of those guys date Trista's gang.

What's that old saying about a rock and a hard place? I think I finally understand it.

CHAPTER FIVE

BEFORE I CAN SHUT the office door behind me, Abby's bouncing in front of my face. I was hoping she'd already left campus without me but no such luck. Her wrist is wrapped in an Ace bandage, but other than that, she looks fine, and I stare at her still-damp baby doll shirt and sparkly jeans, wondering how she can still manage to look cute after the drama at lunch. In my black t-shirt and torn jeans, I look the part of a delinquent. She raises her brows until they almost disappear beneath her hair. Her eyes are wide behind her glasses.

"Well?" she whispers fiercely, looking in both directions down the already deserted hall. She grabs my hand and tugs me close even though it is apparent that we are the only losers left in the hallway twenty minutes after the final bell of the day. I don't know if she's asking about my punishment or Big Betty's injury; either is more than I want to discuss right now. But I'm *really* hoping it's the first one.

"Looks like your arm's not broken after all." I make an attempt at light-hearted good humor. "You feeling okay?" I'm deliberately ignoring her question, hoping to stall since I really haven't had a chance to think of a believable lie. I know Abby saw that girl's extra crispy wrist, and I have no idea what to tell her.

The truth is *not* an option. She'll think I'm completely insane, and she's the only friend I have. I can't lose Abby. I just can't get through every day without her. I'll do what I have to do to keep Abby in the dark even if that means resorting to something I haven't done in a long time and promised myself I would never do again.

"You know very well what I'm talking about! V, what happened? How did you do that to Betty Sanders?" Great, I have to explain the harder of the two. So much for hoping to get by easy.

"Am I like the only person in school who didn't know that girl's name?" I ask, still avoiding.

"Viv! Stop trying to get me off topic! You fried Betty's arm. It was like... red and kinda bubbly." She shutters and screws up her face. "Gross!"

"I didn't do anything to her arm except maybe bruise it, and I seriously doubt that. Did you see the size of her arm? I'd have to be on the weight lifting team to hurt her." I shrug, trying for nonchalance. I walk away, turning my back to her. But she follows me as I walk to my locker and drag out the books I'll need for homework.

"Hello, Viv! I was there. Up close and personal, remember? No one else was close enough to see it or smell it"—she wrinkles her nose, which pushes her glasses up at the same time—"but I was there. Her arm was like smoking, and when you let her go, it wasn't normal." She shakes her head and puts her hand on top on my books.

I hate that word. I've fought to be that very thing my entire life. I know it will never happen, but I have to keep trying. I'm going to have to do some serious damage control. I just hope I only have to do it once, well, maybe twice depending on how much info Betty shares when she returns. I'm kind of counting on Betty's tough girl attitude to keep her from sharing too many details. Then again, that same attitude may keep her on my case for the rest of the year.

I throw everything in my ratty backpack, zip it, and turn around where Abby stands behind me. I shrug and walk away from her toward the main exit. As I push open the glass doors, I catch a glimpse of her stubborn look in the reflection, and I know what I have to do as soon as we get to her car—the thing I really wanted to avoid doing. I'm going to have to alter Abby's memories of the fight.

"You can't avoid my questions forever, V," she says as we walk across the almost empty parking lot. She presses the unlock button on her key ring, and I hear the doors to the loaded Mustang that she got at the beginning of the school year unlock. I open the passenger door, throw my backpack on the plush leather interior of the backseat, and climb into the front while Abby slides behind the wheel a second later. She turns to face me again, lips pursed expectantly.

"We aren't going anywhere until you answer me."

"Sorry, Abby, I didn't want to do this, but you leave me no other choice." I run my fingers through my hair, which I am sure is starting to look greasy after the number of times I've performed this little nervous habit today.

She looks at me strangely, the question evident on her face.

"What do you—" She begins but never finishes because I put one hand on either side of her face. "Viv, why are you holding my face?" We lock eyes, and I can feel that tingle again, only on a smaller, much less scary scale.

"Vivian, what's happening to your eyes?" Abby suddenly gets a spacey look on her face, and I'm inside her mind.

It's a strange sensation hearing someone's thoughts or altering someone's memories. It's kind of like accidentally opening the bathroom door when your brother is getting out of the shower—not that I have or ever have had a brother, but I figure that's got to be awkward and uncomfortable for both parties. I've done this occasionally on some teachers in elementary school to make them reconsider weekend homework and once on a sales girl to get her to accept an out-dated coupon, but never for anything major and definitely never to Abby.

The last time I did this was a little more than two years ago when Aunt Charlotte refused to let me go with Abby and her parents on vacation to Cancun. I wanted to go so badly because I'd never been *anywhere*, and I wanted to go to keep Abby company since she was going to be alone most of the time while her parents did their own thing. So, I really didn't see why Aunt Charlotte was being so mean by not letting me go.

After begging didn't work, I sort of took her brain hostage. I invaded her mind while she was sleeping in order to insert the suggestion that she let me go with Abby and her parents. She would agree and think it was her idea, an abuse of my powers but necessary to get what I wanted. However, when you place a thought, it's impossible not to hear the other person's thoughts at the same time. I not only heard her thoughts; I also saw her dream.

There I was, five years old, auburn hair in sloppy braids I must have done myself, big gray eyes full of tears, and it was like I was right there reliving it all again. Aunt Charlotte was hugging me to her so hard that I actually felt my breath leave my chest. This all happened eleven years ago, right after my mother had been killed, and my child self was seeing my aunt for the first time ever. As my only living relative, she'd shown up immediately to claim me after the authorities contacted her.

"You look so much like Violet, little Vivian," she'd said, looking into my eyes and stroking my cheek. *"Come on, let's go home."*

That's when I pulled my hands away from the still-sleeping Aunt Charlotte. The guilt was overwhelming. This woman, a struggling kindergarten teacher, took me in, supported me, and created a home for me. She moved us from her one-bedroom apartment to an old but homey farmhouse in this town, my only permanent home ever. It was the first time I'd lived in an actual house, not an apartment, hotel, or tent which was about all I could remember of my mother, and here I was trying to hijack her into letting me go on a trip! I promised myself right then never to use my abilities like that again, and today, when I felt Betty's fear, was the first time I'd even come close since then.

Now, I was going to do the thing I'd sworn not to do to my closest—my only—friend. Crap, crap, crap! Crap to infinity!

I didn't want to stay too long in Ab's head, both out of consideration and out of fear at what I might see. I mean there are just some things I don't want to know about ANYBODY. I didn't want to take a chance on seeing some embarrassing image that would be forever burned into my brain. A quiet in and out operation so to speak.

From what I can tell from my limited experience, everyone's brain is set up differently. Sometimes it's easy to make suggestions; sometimes it's a little more trying. Some people seem to have a filing cabinet memory storage system; those are the easy ones to manipulate. They readily accept your suggestions into their minds as long as it all fits in the labeled folders their brains have set up for them. Then there are the more free spirits with little puffy-cloud thoughts that you have to reach out and grab, liking the carnival game with the little rubber ducks. You just keep picking them up until you find what you want, and Abby's mind is the latter but more adorable.

Her mind is peaceful, sunny sky, birds chirping—very fairytale, princess movie. It just confirms that she's so not tough and hard like she wants everyone to believe, the exact reason I have to protect her from people like Trista and, if I am being totally honest, from people like me, too.

Her thoughts and memories grow like flowers. I locate the scene from lunch today and begin to alter it by telling her she never saw smoke or smelled anything except the beans in the cafeteria. I tell her she only saw red marks on Betty's arm, red marks that will become bruises, not blisters, and definitely not burns. If there are any burns, they were already there when she approached us. Then I hightail it out of there by jerking my hands from her face.

As Abby wakes from the fog, I say, "So you see, Ab, it was totally self-defense, and I didn't mean to cause those bruises." I do this knowing she won't remember what just happened and hoping that she doesn't ask more questions so that I don't have to go back into her mind.

She shakes her head, trying to clear away the haze, and straightens her glasses where my hands left them a little crooked. "Uh… yeah, of course not, V. I just wanted to hear it from your viewpoint."

She still looks a little confused, uncertain of the conversation we just had, and I feel guilty and completely ashamed of myself when she starts the car and takes me home.

CHAPTER SIX

I CLOSE ABBY'S CAR DOOR and wave goodbye as she backs out of the driveway and heads to the three-story house where she lives with her part-time parents. Abby's house is in the good part of town, where people water their lawns and give their dogs pedicures. Her house looks like something staged for a magazine shoot, and it's just about as empty. What good are a pool, sauna, media room, and a shower big enough to do cartwheels inside if no one is there to share it with you?

Abby's life is full of 'stuff', expensive luxurious stuff. She's more like a well-kept pet than a daughter. Personally, I'll take our run-down, shabby farmhouse over that mausoleum where she lives any day. My house may be old with a sagging veranda porch and chipped white paint, but it's warm, and I don't mean in the temperature sense of the word.

Aunt Charlotte and I are more than just blood relatives like Abby and her parents. Aunt Charlotte isn't really my aunt. She's my cousin, but she and my mother grew up together like sisters, raised by their grandmother. After my mother was killed, I came to live with Aunt Charlotte because she's my only known living relative. We're just as close as mother and daughter, though, more so than Abby and her mom.

Aunt Charlotte and I live outside of town about five miles, the house is nestled in a small forest and surrounded by little farms. As I walk up to the front door I notice Aunt Charlotte's old car parked in the usual spot next to the house. I pull my cell phone from my back pocket and look at the clock. She's earlier than usual. Great, that probably means Mr. Sailers called her, and she came right home after school. I brace myself for impact and open the front door.

I let the screen door slam shut behind me and look around our living room at the drafty windows, the worn hardwood floors with the old multi-colored rope rugs, the furniture that has seen better days, and the shade-tree green walls covered with family photos in mismatched frames. *This* is a home, maybe a little dusty because I haven't gotten around to my chores this week. But right now, it's just way too quiet. There's no TV on, no humming from the laundry room while Aunt Charlotte sorts the clothes, and no chopping, dicing, or sizzling from the kitchen.

"Aunt Charlotte? Where are you?" I toss my bag on the floor, walk into the hall, and glance inside Aunt Charlotte's bedroom, the spare bedroom, the bathroom, and the kitchen.

"Aunt Charlotte, are you upstairs?" I stop to call up the narrow staircase leading to what should be the attic but has been converted into my own spacious bedroom and bathroom.

Well, that leaves only one alternative, the place Aunt Charlotte goes when she's most upset—the garden. That's just freakin' wonderful! If she's gardening on a school night, she's pissed. It's not unusual to see her out there on her knees digging all weekend but hardly ever on a school night because she's typically too busy preparing for the next school day. Yet there she is, floppy hat perched on her long, curly red ponytail, old man overalls she got at a yard sale, and flowered gloves that dwarf her tiny hands. Lately, since my recent visits in the principal's office, I've seen her out there more than she should have been in December when the ground was nearly frozen solid.

I glance out the back door. She is bent over a huge basket full of plants and bulbs. As I walk outside and close in on the garden plot, I see all the shallow holes she's already dug, and I wonder just how angry she is if she's worked that quickly. In the summer this area will be full of veggies, flowers, and melons, and I'll have picking duty added to my chores. I really don't mind because I love the produce, and I love the idea of helping Aunt Charlotte with something she takes pride in doing.

"Hey, you're home early. No afterschool tutoring tonight?" Aunt Charlotte stays late three nights a week to tutor the students who need a little more help. If she didn't stay, this is really not good.

"No, Vivian, I cancelled tutoring this afternoon." She stops the movement of her spade and raises her eyes to mine. "After I got a call from your principal." Her eyes bore into mine. Aunt Charlotte and I resemble each other, but that crystal blue glare is all her own. I feel a tiny bit sorry for her kindergartners.

I drop my gaze first.

"What happened?" Her voice is tired and disappointed. "No wait," she holds up her hand in a motion that stops the words in my throat and causes me to close my mouth. As she gets up and dusts off her knees, I turn and head for the house, the kitchen table to be exact. That's our gathering place. We probably spend more time in that room than in any other (except for sleeping, of course). Charlotte is a great cook; she can whip up a mouth-watering meal from the simplest, cheapest ingredients, a talent that she's honed from all these years being, essentially, a single mom trying to live on a teacher's salary. She makes the best everything! Me, not so much. The last time I cooked dinner, we ended up ordering a pizza since I can't cook. I do the cleaning and some of the laundry.

After I enter the kitchen, I sit at the table and pick at the tear in the thigh of my jeans while Aunt Charlotte washes her hands. She sighs deeply, a sound I seem to be hearing from adults a little too often lately. The water stops, and she turns, drying her hands on a small, holey kitchen towel.

"Now go." As she leans against the counter, I recount my day beginning with the good grade and ending when I walked away from Betty in the cafeteria. I leave out the part about the smoking skin, hoping she'll just think it was all a normal fight.

She keeps a blank look throughout my tale, but when I finish, she says, "This girl was a giant, huh? And you forced her to the ground? Vivian, you used your powers didn't you?"

"Kinda," I mumble, looking down again. Here it comes, the explosion sure to be heard all the way to town. Her ratty tennis shoes and lower legs approach the table, and her hand is on my back. She squats down eye-level with me, and I finally look at her.

"Did you do it on purpose?" She runs the tip of her tongue along the tight seam of her lips and waits expectantly.

"No, I swear, Aunt Charlotte!" I shake my head and put out my hands, palms up to emphasize my point.

"She was huge, a flippin' mountain compared to Ab and me! When she grabbed Abby, I knew she was really going to hurt her, and something inside of me sort of, I don't know, snapped. I know you've always told me not to use my powers, but I just couldn't help it!" I pause. Here goes the bad part. "I might've cooked her arm a teeny weeny bit." I hurry on, "Really, it wasn't even noticeable..." I trail off because my throat gets tight as tears flood my eyes. Crap! I hate crying. I make it a point not to cry, ever. Crying shows weakness, and weakness puts an enormous target on your back.

She rubs my arm. "It's okay, Vivian. I think we need to have a chat, though." We talk all the time right here at this table about school or books or whatever. The last time we had a 'chat', however, I was ten, and after the chat ended, I swore I'd never even kiss a boy much less do what she'd just told me about. She takes the seat across from me.

"Vivian, how much do you remember about your mom's abilities?" Her eyes are troubled, and there are little worry lines across her forehead.

I rack my brain for the tiny scraps of memory I have of my mother. "Not a lot. I remember she once cooked a couple of hot dogs just by touching them. She did that little glowing ball thing when we needed a flashlight. Once she had to jump start our car battery. That's pretty much it."

"She could do so much more, Viv. You know that Violet and I grew up together living with our Grandmother Viloula and that Violet's mother, your grandmother, was killed young, too. But I've never talked much about her gift because I wanted to discourage you from using yours. I realize now that that might have been unfair to you." She touches my hand. "I just thought that if we didn't glorify your mom's gift—*your* gift—that I could keep you safe and give you a chance at having a regular life."

She stops talking for a second. "I think I need a drink." She stands and takes a small glass from the cabinet where we keep the dishes. Then she moves to the tiny cabinet above the stove's vent hood. That cabinet is so minuscule I thought it was empty. I've never seen Aunt Charlotte take anything from it, and since I don't want to poison us and never cook, I definitely haven't ever opened it. On tiptoes she reaches far back in the cabinet and pulls out a bottle of whiskey. She turns back to the table and immediately pours a small amount in the glass. I am beyond shocked.

"Vivian, if your eyes get any bigger, they'll pop right out of your head." She chuckles and sips.

"Aunt Charlotte, WTF?" My voice rises a little.

"Language," But she smiles. "Oh lighten up! I'm not an alcoholic or anything. So what were we talking about? Oh yeah, Violet."

She settles into her chair. "You already know your gift is inherited through the females in the family, but not all of us inherit it as you also know." She pauses and sips. "My mother, your grandmother's twin sister, didn't inherit either which left her angry and very resentful. That's why she dumped me with Grandma Lou and took off. Your grandmother, Veronica, died in her twenties, shortly after her husband." When she pauses to sip this time, I interrupt.

"What's up with all the 'V' names anyway?"

"I don't know. Your mom once asked Grandma Lou the same question, and Grandma said when your 'gifted' child is born, the name just comes into your head, almost like the baby tells you the name"—she shrugs—"just another part of this ability. Grandma Lou didn't know much about where or how the gift originated. She said it dated at least to colonial times but that with each generation the power seems to increase. Grandma said the power comes from electricity, electromagnetic fields, on the Earth. She said electricity is all around us, in the air, the ground, even our own bodies. I don't really understand it all, and I don't think your great-grandmother did either. She always thought it was best to just accept it and not question it too much."

She stops, and still clutching her glass, rises from the table to pace between the stove and the fridge. I want her to keep talking, so I speak up. "I already knew most of that. What else do you know?"

"When your mom was fifteen, Grandma Lou helped her 'charge,'" she says, using the air quote thing. "All of those females who inherit the power are born with a small amount of it already. As children they can do minor things like light up a light bulb or give tiny shocks. That was your mom's favorite pastime when we were kids. For a while I couldn't turn my back on her without getting a surprise jolt to my behind." Her smile is so sad it breaks my heart, and I can almost see the two of them as children, a tiny brunette skipping beside an even tinier redhead. She sits and pulls my attention back to the now. "But when the child comes of age, old enough to use the power responsibly, she is taken by an old pro, a woman who has her power already, and given her first charge to fully manifest the power. Once Violet received her first charge, she was so powerful! She could do amazing things!" She pauses and jumps up quickly. "Wait here." Her eyes are alight as she jogs out of the room.

When she returns, she's holding a photo that I recognize from the living room wall. It's a teenage Charlotte with my mom. They both have braces, and Charlotte's hair is short and curly while my mom has long, brown hair and black sunglasses. They're both so happy, hugging each other cheek-to-cheek, standing in front of a lake sparkling in the sunshine. I've seen this photo a million times, but the only real thought I've ever given it is how goofy Charlotte looks with that haircut and how I wish I were as cool as my mom looks. I've never considered the two girls immortalized there.

"This is the lake where Grandma Lou took Violet to help her manifest her power. I remember what a horrible, stormy night it was and how worried I was that Grandma didn't know what she was doing."

"So" — I look at her in confusion — "how have I always been able to do so many things if I'm supposed to be charged by a powered-up female when I am 'of age?'" Now she has me doing the air quotes. "Shouldn't I just have received my full powers in the last year or so? And who plugged me in anyway? Every female with power is dead, right?" All this talk about power and charging is making me feel like a dead battery.

"That we know of, yes. That's where I'm headed with all of this. Your mother left Grandma Lou's when she turned eighteen. I was a couple of years younger and still in school, so I stayed behind and missed her so much I thought I would die. Violet met a guy and just gradually stopped calling home." She sits at the table again, her eyes on the glass in front of her.

"You mean my dad, whoever that is." I try to keep the bitterness out of my voice, but I fail miserably — maybe I wasn't trying all that hard. I don't even know my dad's name.

"Yeah, all I know about him is she met him at a restaurant where she was waitressing while she was taking some classes at a community college somewhere out west I think. She came back here, to the South, and contacted me when Grandma Lou died. She told me she was pregnant, but I didn't hear from her again until right before her death."

Aunt Charlotte takes a shuttering breath. "Someone was after the two of you, and she was running. She was actually on her way to bring you to me when she was killed. She wanted to keep you hidden and safe and knew it was only a matter of time before they caught up with her." Tears slip down her cheeks leaving thin trails in the dust on them, and she smears it more when she swipes the tears away with the back of her hand.

"I have no idea who was after her or what happened right before she was killed, but she must have charged your power because you came to me manifesting your full power. She must have been desperate because she took a huge risk giving a five-year-old girl that kind of power." She shakes her head thoughtfully. "Think about the problems we could have had…," she says trailing off, and we sit quietly for a minute.

"Wow, this is a lot to take in. Why tell me this now? Just to make me feel better after what I did today?"

"Yes and no. I've always feared whoever killed your mom would find you. That's why I moved us here. I wanted to keep you safe. She died to protect you, and I would never let anything happen to you." She reaches over and tucks a lock of hair behind my ear. "Vivian, you're like my own child, and I'm so afraid that these people will find you, too. Your mom never came out and explained how they found her, but she did say she thought they somehow traced her power. That's one of the reasons I have always cautioned you about yours. I don't know how they can do that, whether it's some kind of machine or"—she flounders for the word and looks up at the ceiling as if it is printed there—"just plain old gossip. I don't know! What if someone catches you using it and puts a video online or mentions it in some blog? It's my job to keep you safe, honey."

And because I don't know what else to do, I get up and pull her to me in a crushing hug. "Thank you, Aunt Charlotte," I say, pulling away from her. "I forget all that you've given up and done for me.

I'm so sorry about the fight today, and I'll be super careful from now on. I promise."

She wipes the tears from her cheeks and smiles. "Be who you are, Vivian, but be cautious, okay?"

"One more little thing, Aunt Charlotte. Uh... I kinda had to... to change Abby's memory a tiny bit." I hold up my thumb and forefinger close together. "And I'll be late getting home starting... well.... starting tomorrow, actually, because I have to tutor some jock as my punishment. Oh! And I don't want to ask Abby to wait, sooo you'll have to come pick me up." I say all of this rapidly in a rambling fashion and smile crookedly, hoping she doesn't think she made a mistake in taking me in all those years ago.

CHAPTER SEVEN

THE SKY IS DARK. A strong wind grabs at my face. My hair has come loose from my braids and is dancing around my head like reddish-brown flames. My feet are wet inside my white sneakers. My jeans are heavy with water and tug tightly at my waist. The wind rushing up the back of my shirt. I squish my toes together as another wave washes over the riverbank where I'm standing. Thunder booms loudly overhead as jagged lightning forks to the ground in the distance.

My mother is squeezing my hand hard, and I hear her whisper-thin voice inside of my head even though her lips never move, and her eyes still search the sky.

Any minute now, baby girl.

Her face is that of the photo minus the sunglasses, aged only slightly from that moment with Aunt Charlotte. Goose bumps snake down my arms; the tiny hairs tingle.

I feel like someone is watching me, so I glance around at the lopsided tent we tried to set up and at our car, out of gas again, parked by the path that runs through the woods.

What had my mother said earlier to the woman crying on the other end of the payphone? Something about a man, something about danger.

When the thunder breaks this time, the sound steals my breath and makes me jump. Then mother reaches out her hands, and the lightning leaps toward her.

* * *

I wake with a start and look at my open window where rain is blowing in, soaking my floor. My alarm clock shows 6:23am, almost time to get up anyway. Throwing back the covers, I stumble out of bed and close the window against the pre-spring storm. It's going to be one of those days, I can already tell.

In the bathroom I study my face in the mirror above the sink. I look so much like her, my mom. It's strange, resembling someone you really don't even know. All that stuff Aunt Charlotte threw at me last night makes me more curious to know what happened to her, to find my dad if he's out there. Then I remember the dream that awakened me just minutes ago. It's the first time I've had that dream in years. I used to have it all the time, nearly every night when I first came to live with Aunt Charlotte. When I was little, it would scare me. I'd wake up shaking, and Aunt Charlotte would crawl in bed with me, singing softly until I relaxed again.

This time something is different, though. I try to run my hand through my hair, but it's too tangled, and my fingers snag on the knotted mess, so I step into the shower with the dream still on my mind. What was different? That difference is important. I feel it. I shake my head. Maybe it's just one of those weird dream things where the images are distorted, like when you dream about your house, but there's a freaky clown guy in his underwear eating cereal in the living room. Alright, maybe not quite that weird, but you get my point.

Throughout my usual morning routine of wash, dry, brush, I mull it over. The dream was so sharp, so vivid this time. I've never really felt the wind and water like I did this time. The images were so real. Maybe it has something to do with the storm outside, or maybe it's just because Aunt Charlotte and I talked about my mother for so long last night.

After I dress in a red t-shirt and dark-wash jeans, I gather my homework that is still spread out on the couch from the night before. Aunt Charlotte and I talked so late that I didn't begin my Calculus worksheet until after we ate our supper of grilled burgers. As I throw my binder and books into my backpack, I feel as though I've forgotten something. When I grab my library book, it hits me.

Book talks are today in English. I totally forgot to write out some notes. Crap! I'll have to do it on the way to school since English is first period. It's bad enough to be prepared and get up there in front of the class to tell about a book. If I go up there with nothing, I'll choke with all those eyes watching me. That's it! The part of the dream that was nagging me. Someone had been watching my mom and me that day beside the river. I was looking for them behind us. But who was it?

* * *

"Just call my name already," I mumble to myself as I listen to the kid finishing his book talk.

"And if you want to know what happens to the alien forces on Jupiter, you'll have to read the book." Manly Jenkins's voice is the most annoying sound in the world. Nails on a chalkboard, a dentist's drill, a car alarm in the middle of the night—these have nothing on Manly. What a dumb name anyway. Who chooses an adjective as their kid's name? And 'manly'? Wow, could you set the kid up any harder for failure? Manly Jenkins is anything but his namesake. In fact, he is the exact opposite, a walking oxymoron. Short, scrawny, and feminine, that pretty much sums him up. But he is undeniably smart, the person to beat if I chose to compete. I almost choke every time I let him outscore me because I know it would be so easy to overtake him, be the top of the junior class, and wipe off that superior look he always has.

A few polite kids, a group in which I am *not* included, applaud as he returns to his seat with his patent smirking half-smile. He glances at me, and I covertly scratch my cheek with my middle finger. He gets the message, shakes his head like I'm too immature for him, and faces forward, hands folded on his desk. Ugh! I can't stand that guy.

Finally, Mrs. Crafton calls me up to the front. The book talk goes okay, and the bell for second hour rings.

As I'm collecting my belongings, Mrs. Crafton asks, "Vivian, could you stay a minute?"

I give her the what-did-I-do look, and she adds, "You're not in trouble. I just want to talk to you about your tutoring assignment."

She is gathering papers and putting them into an already stuffed manila folder.

Everyone files out, and we are alone for a minute while the halls fill with bodies and voices.

"Mr. Sailers asked me to get together some work for you and the boy you're tutoring. I have a folder of worksheets and assignments that Easton needs to do to raise his grade."

I nod and accept the bulging folder, using both hands to keep everything in. This will take forever—excellent, wonderful, freakin' awesome. I may have to do some of this for... What was his name? Easton? I'd like to be done by, oh I don't know, August!

She's nodding and saying something. I jerk back into the conversation, nod my head as though I've been listening, and smile. I like Mrs. Crafton. She always tries to make class interesting but pushes us to do our best, and I don't want to hurt her feelings or make her mad, so I have to make the best of this mess I've made. After all, it isn't her fault I nearly set a kid on fire, even if the Neanderthal deserved it.

She scribbles me a note in case I'm late for second hour. As I turn to leave, I see a few kids coming into the room. I realize this must be senior English. Since I'm not a social butterfly, I don't know any of them. When I reach the door, Mrs. Crafton calls my name, and I turn toward her.

"As he finishes the work, he needs to turn it in so that I can grade it and reenter his grades into the computer, okay?" She nods and raises her eyebrows to make sure I understand. Her glasses slide lower on her nose in her patented look.

"Okay, Mrs. Crafton. See you tomorrow." I sling my backpack over my shoulder.

When I turn back around, I smack smooth into a wall of chest, a hard, great-smelling male chest. The full folder goes crashing to the floor, and the papers scatter as if they are trying to make a run for it. I catch a glimpse of a blue button-up shirt as I drop to my knees to gather the papers.

"Oh, sorry!" I inwardly cursing my embarrassing clumsiness. Why couldn't I have run over Manly instead of the cute guy? I haven't looked at him yet, but anyone who smells like he does with a chest that hard must be hot.

"No, it's my fault. You okay?" A voice as rich and smooth as melted chocolate caresses my ears. Eyes still down, I see Mrs. Crafton hurrying over to help, her pointy shoes clattering on the tile floor.

As we gather the papers, a well-shaped, masculine hand brushes mine, and a charge shoots up my entire arm, leaving goose bumps and a slight tremor in its wake. The force is not painful, but it's so strong that I gasp, jerk my hand back, and look up into the most beautiful male face I've ever seen. His strong chin and jaw are covered in barely-there, dark stubble. His nose is straight, and his skin is the color of coffee with cream, complimenting hair as black as sin, but what draws me are his eyes, aquamarine like a tropical lagoon, and all I want to do is take a swim in them.

"Oh wow, did I shock you? Sorry about that. That kinda hurt, huh?" He's rubbing his fingers on the hand that touched mine. Then he smiles, and wow, just... wow. It's like a movie moment in one of those chick flicks Aunt Charlotte loves. Boy meets girl, and girl can't remember her name.

I must look like a total moron gawking at him with my mouth hanging open slightly. I drop my eyes, and try to run my hand through my hair before I remember I have it in a messy bun today.

"No, I mean, yes, you shocked me, but no, it didn't hurt." Geez, could I sound any dumber? "I'm fine."

I lose my balance a little and have to drop my hand to the tile floor to keep from falling over. He reaches out one hand to my shoulder to help steady me, and I feel it again through my shirt, so intense this time I shudder; an actual shudder runs through my entire body, and I close my eyes at the sensation. What the hell is wrong with me?

This time he jerks away as if he's been burned. Shit! Did I just zap him? He looks at his hand, turning it over twice, and we both look up at the same time. Cool aquamarine meets smoky gray. Am I sweating?

Mrs. Crafton's gaze slides between the two of us, and her mouth turns up slightly at one corner in a conspiratorial smile.

"Vivian Cartwright, meet Easton Garrett. Easton, meet Vivian, your new tutor.

CHAPTER EIGHT

AS ABBY AND I ENTER the cafeteria for the first time since our encounter, all eyes turn to us. Abby stops and squares her shoulders. She turns to me for support. I nod, and we start across the room to our table. Whispers swirl around us; a few jerks even point. But after we sit and take out our lunches the volume increases to normal, and everybody turns back to their own tablemates.

"So, how's your day been? You seemed upset on the way to school this morning," Abby says, dipping her spoon into her blueberry yogurt. Her hair is pulled back in a ponytail, and her glasses are pushed up on her forehead. She's wearing a blue t-shirt and yoga-style pants, her comfort clothes. She usually dresses to impress. Her slob clothes only make an appearance when she's sick or stressed, so she must be upset today. It could be because of the rain that's been falling since early this morning, but I'll bet that's not all. The attention from our little problem must be weighing on her, another reason to shun the freaks and another step away from the popularity she craves.

"I didn't sleep very well last night." I lie just so I don't have to relive the dream. "I also had that stupid book talk first hour, too." I unwrap my PB and J and take a bite. A glob plops on the front of my shirt. Wonderful. At least my shirt is a dark color and won't show the stain too badly.

"Oh, I forgot to tell you! I met the new boy. He *is* a junior, *and* he's in my study hall. His name is Dillenger Wescott. That's him over there." She points with her spoon to a tall guy with brown hair and a 'You want me and I know it' walk. His stylish, ripped jeans and the flipped up collar on his orange polo-style shirt scream attitude. She's right; he is definitely attractive, but there is something almost slimy about him. His eyes look hard and jaded even from this distance.

He approaches the dime squad table, and Darcy Fletcher, Trista's best friend, scoots over to make room for him at the end of the table. She pats the seat next to her, and her giggle travels across the room to us. She tosses her light brown hair over the shoulder that's exposed by the asymmetrical top she's wearing. I raise an eyebrow at Abby as she takes out her ham sandwich and pulls off the crust.

"I didn't actually talk to him yet. But tomorrow I am definitely going to. He smiled and winked at me when he sat down in study hall today." She is so excited, her eyes lit with the hope that he might want her, that I can't bring myself to state the obvious. If he's been here a day and is already sitting with them, I'm pretty sure he's a lost cause for her, considering how much they hate us. I doubt he'll be blowin' up her phone with texts, and as soon as he discovers we're often the punch line to their pranks, he won't even acknowledge her anymore. As she nibbles the sandwich, I can't help feeling guilty again. Poor Abby craves attention and not the kind she gets from having me as a friend.

"Speaking of meeting new guys, I met the guy I'm tutoring this morning. Truthfully, I ran over him coming out of Mrs. Crafton's room." I'm trying to sound indifferent, but my excitement can't be contained, and I grin idiotically thinking of those eyes and the literal shock he made me feel.

"Oh yeah, who is he? More importantly, what's he look like? Judging from the look on your face, I'm guessin' he's cute." She wiggles her eyebrows up and down, grinning, as she slips the tiny plastic straw into her juice pouch.

"Abby, he is so hot! And I made a complete ass of myself. Why am I so hopeless?" I drop my half-eaten sandwich because suddenly I've lost my appetite, remembering I must have looked like a complete loser in his eyes, those gorgeous eyes that I would gladly drown in.

"What's his name? If he's hot, I probably know him." And since Abby has a mental yearbook of every attractive guy since seventh grade, I figure she's probably right.

"Easton Garrett." Sighing, I gaze absently out the windows where the rain still sluices down.

Abby spews a mouthful of juice. "What! Did you say Easton Garrett?" Her eyes are huge; apparently she does recognize the name.

Looking at her, I raise my eyebrows and tilt my head toward her. "Yeah, why? Is that bad?"

"Bad? Yeah, 'bad' is a good word for it. 'Holy crap' fits a little more accurately, though!" I glance around the cafeteria and see some white-faced goths at the table closest to us are looking in Abby's direction.

"Got a problem?" I glare back at them. Abby's reaction has thrown me and left me a little on edge. Why is she freakin' out?

As they turn back around, Abby faces me again and takes a deep breath. "V, how is it possible you don't know who that is? He's the guy that enrolled when school started back after Christmas break." The way she's looking at me makes me feel lame and clueless.

"Still drawing a blank here, Ab," I say shaking my head.

"He's the baseball guy, the one who moved here to play for Coach Wilson in the spring. He's like almost a pro or something. Black hair, amazing body? I told you about him!" She smacks my arm, and a wounded frown creases her forehead and crinkles her eyes.

"I can't keep up with all the guys you talk about." I rub my stinging forearm. "I love you, chica, but when you talk boys, I just zone out sometimes. Sorry."

I'm trying to be gentle, but Abby is boy-crazy. Every guy that comes along catches her eye. She's never been on a real date; neither of us has, but that doesn't stop her from window shopping every boy she sees.

When I look away to the side door, I see him. There he is in his blue shirt left untucked, his rolled sleeves, and his jeans with rips in all the right places. How did I not notice him before now? I can't help but sigh and drool but only a little bit.

Abby's 'guy dar' hones in on him like a heat-seeking missile. Then she's drooling, too; we may need a mop over here soon at this rate.

"He's so pretty," she says dreamily. "Why can't I be his tutor?"

"Because you didn't fight with the sasquatch girl, Abby." She looks at me, and we both laugh. She picks at the bread on her sandwich.

"True, V. By the way, she's back." She opens her pudding and takes out a spoon.

"Who?" I'm having trouble concentrating because I'm all warm and fuzzy from watching Easton walk over to the jock table carrying a tray and some sort of juice bottle.

"Betty Sanders, I saw her heading into Sailers' office this morning," she says around a mouthful of chocolate pudding.

"Thanks for the warning." I gather what's left of my sandwich and napkin. Dealing with her won't be a picnic, but it'll all work out. My stomach twists. I'll make sure it does by whatever means necessary—even if that means a trip into her mind.

Abby nods in the direction of the jock table where Easton has just taken a seat. "You do know who's after him, right?"

"No, but I'll bet you're gonna tell me." I take a drink from my water bottle with one hand and secretly check my phone in my lap with the other. We aren't supposed to have our phones out at school, but everyone still does it. I don't know why I bother checking, though. Besides Aunt Charlotte, the only person who ever texts is sitting right next to me.

"You don't know this either? Geez, Viv, like, you've gotta pay attention more." She points to the dime squad table where Trista has just scooted out her chair. She stands, hikes up her jean skirt, and jerks at the bottom of her top, causing her v-neck sweater to land precisely where her overworked push-up bra exposes her cleavage. Rubbing her gloss-saturated lips together, she saunters over to the jock table, one hip at a time. Her tall boots add to her overall 'worship my sexiness' slink. She stops beside Easton's chair and bends low to whisper in his ear, nearly spilling her boobs onto his shoulder. A total accident, I'm so sure!

Abby returns the sympathetic smile I've given her about a million times when she gushes about some guy she thinks might be 'the one.' "Trista's already staked her claim," she says, patting my hand in that soothing gesture your mom would use when you've had a bad day.

The hand that had been holding my phone suddenly emanates warmth. I turn it over and in my palm see a gleaming streak of blue.

CHAPTER NINE

THE 3:20 BELL RINGS, and I have a headache. After the day I've had, all I want to do is go home, put on my jammies, and crawl under the quilt Great-Grandma Lou made for Charlotte.

Yeah, that's not gonna happen. I have my first tutoring session in about ten minutes. Mr. S arranged for Easton and me to meet in a study area of the library. As nervous as I am, I still can't wait to see him again, but the nagging pain in my head dampens that excitement. Between my Spanish homework and the lab report I have for chemistry, I need to work on my on homework, not babysit for an hour, even if the baby is six-plus feet with kiss-worthy lips.

Right after lunch Abby informed my socially-challenged self that while Trista and Easton are not officially a couple yet, they will be. At least that's the rumor. She never loses, and if she's set her sights on him, it won't take long. How could he NOT want her? Perfection is perfection even when it's shallow. Boys like girls like Trista; they don't tend to care much about personality when it's wrapped in looks like hers. Life doesn't work out like it does on television, where the quiet girl wins the guy.

"It's inevitable, Viv. Could you resist those boobs if you were a guy? I seriously doubt it." She just shrugs as though it's common knowledge and unavoidable.

"You make it sound like I'm after him. I wouldn't stand a chance with that kind of guy, and I have no aspirations of getting him. I'm not even thinking about asking him out nor am I delusional enough to think he'd ask me. Can't I just like looking at him?"

"Of course you can. What girl wouldn't want to look at him? Who knows, V? If the stars align and you really, really believe"—she grabs both of my hands and pulls them close under her chin while she bats her eyes—"you could live happily ever after, have a million babies, a cat, and a dog." She laughs.

I give her a look that tells her I am not amused and jerk my hands from hers. "Funny, Ab. Yeah, and the devil might show up selling ice skates."

That was several hours ago, and I've thought of nothing else since. I couldn't concentrate in US history and probably made a 'B' or 'C' on the quiz over Gettysburg. After the final bell stops shrieking, I sling my backpack over one shoulder and head for the library. I pull out my phone to text Abby and tell her I'll call her later when for the second time today I slam into someone, only this time it's not radiant blue-green eyes I see. Instead, the eyes are almost black, and the nose, eyebrows, and lips are pierced. Taking a deep breath, I step back from Betty Sanders without even being aware I'm doing it.

"Hey there… Betty," I stammer, trying to think of what to say to the girl I almost turned into a human torch. "Glad to see you're okay?" It comes out a question, and any minute now she's going to pound me into the scuffed tile the way villains do on cartoons; there will only be a Vivian puddle left. There is no sign of my power, not even a tingle. Bet Superman never had this problem.

She continues to glare as she crosses her arms over her massive girth. This girl must shop at Convicts R Us, black psycho band t-shirt with the sleeves cut off, black vinyl pants (Who wears vinyl?), and a nearly floor-length chain draped from her front left pocket to her back left pocket. From the spiky hair to the biker boots, she radiates intensity. She'd make a great extra on a post-apocalyptic, zombie movie.

She closes the gap I just made between us, and I glance at the bandage wrapped around her wrist.

"How did you do this?" She holds up her arm as if I could've missed it. Her eyes are squinty like I'm an insect she's studying to find the right angle to squish me.

"Listen, Betty. I'm sorry, alright? You were attacking Abby and me. I didn't set out to hurt you, and believe me I wish it hadn't happened." I hold up my hands, palms out, and she does something I never expected. She steps back, not one step but two. At first her reaction confuses me then it hits me like a cement truck. She's afraid of me! How great is this!

Any rational person would take this opportunity to walk away or to continue to make nice, nice with the giant, but I'm not feeling particularly left-brain oriented this afternoon. A thrill travels up my spine. Wonder how far she'll let me take this?

I step toward her; she steps back. Again, I step forward; she retreats. This is fun. We continue our weird dance half-way down the hallway. By then, I'm smiling; I just can't help myself. When my phone beeps a message alert from Abby, I notice that I only have three minutes to meet Easton.

"As much as I'm enjoying our little visit, Betty, I've gotta go." And without hesitation I put my hands on either side of her face. "Don't worry; this'll hurt me more than it'll hurt you." Taking a deep breath, I open her mind.

CHAPTER TEN

BY THE TIME I REACH the library door, I am officially late. Betty's brain was a mess, no surprise there. I couldn't completely wipe out the fight, of course, because too many people saw it. But I did convince her she'd burned her arm before school on her motorcycle muffler. I took a chance with that, but luckily she didn't challenge the new memory which must mean she does have a bike. Shocking, I know.

Easton's already sitting at the round table nestled behind the last bookshelf.

"Sorry," I say as I approach him, making sure to avoid eye contact. "I ran into a problem I had to deal with first."

"It's okay. I just got here a few minutes ago anyway." He's looking at me; I can feel those eyes. Glancing anywhere but at him, I pull his folder from my backpack. I'm digging in the front pocket trying to find a pen when he reaches over and hands me one.

"Thanks," I mumble, and as I take the pen, our fingers brush. Just like this morning, my hand tingles. I finally glance up at him through my lashes, and his eyes are serious, an unspoken question there. He *must* have felt that. His forehead crinkles, and his brows bunch together.

"I, uh, really appreciate this." Now it's his turn to glance down. "I'm sure you've got a million other things you'd rather be doing than helping me. Just warning you, I really suck at English." He laughs nervously, giving me the courage to raise my head and look him fully in the face. Wait, why's he nervous? He looks back at me. Dang, he is supremely hot.

"Mr. Sailers told me this isn't exactly a volunteer job for you. I, uh, was in the cafeteria at lunch yesterday." He quirks the corner of his lips up in an uncertain smile.

I squint my eyes closed in a pained expression. As I open them, I mentally review all those faces scattered around the tables during my little 'episode' and realize he was there with the jocks. But he wasn't smiling with the rest of the kids. I feel the need to explain myself for some reason.

"You saw that? Not my most stellar moment. That was my first" —I raise my fists and shake them a little—"girl fight. Any fight. Fight of any kind, I mean. I don't fight." I'm totally messing this up. I rub my forehead, cursing my awkwardness. Geez, could I possibly sound any lamer? I gift him with a sick smile, but he looks serious. I hurry on. "I'm really not like that."

"I know," he says. "I've seen you around school, and you don't seem like that at all." Then he gives me his first genuine grin, and I almost pass out! He's noticed me? Really? My heartbeat speeds up just thinking about him watching me. I must have a strange expression because he holds up his hand and stops smiling.

"Not in a stalker way! I just realized how creepy that sounds. I only mean I've seen you, like in the hall and stuff. I'm not crazy or anything." He laughs. Maybe he's as nervous as I am after all. "Kind of like I sound right now." And this time his smile is contagious because I smile, too.

I can't believe this Adonis, this photographer's dream specimen, is actually nervous, awkward even, while he's talking to me. My fear starts to subside when he offers me a stick of gum.

"Want some gum? I had the tacos for lunch, and I wouldn't recommend them. I'd hate to knock out my hot new tutor with my breath." He's still grinning when he pops the gum into his very mouth. My eyes linger on his full lips until I force myself to look away, but of their own accord, my eyes go back to him.

He thinks I'm hot? He could just be saying that to butter me up since I am kind of in control of his grade at the moment. But do I really care? Not, at all. He can flatter me *all day long*. I can feel my cheeks turning pink. Once I drag my gaze away, I open the folder, and we spend the next hour completing worksheets on subordinate clauses.

After an hour and a half, I close the folder and try to hand him back his pen.

"Keep it," he says, while he tosses the completed worksheets into his canvas messenger bag. I check my phone and find a message from Aunt Charlotte. Frowning, I read the text informing me that she had an emergency teachers' meeting that will run until 6:00.

"Great." I sigh and begin typing a response, telling her I'll call Abby to see if she can pick me up.

"What's wrong?" Easton stands and puts his bag over his shoulder cross body. It pulls his shirt tight against his chest, emphasizing the muscles there.

"Huh?" I'm staring like an idiot. Way to be smooth, Vivian.

He smiles that crooked smile I'm starting to like and says, "Is there something wrong?" He points to the phone still in my hand, reply unsent.

"Oh, right! No, it's my aunt. She can't pick me up as expected, so I'll have to call Abby." I try not to sound like a pathetic, carless loser even though I am.

"I could give you a ride." He shrugs those impossibly wide shoulders.

"What? Uh, no, I mean you, uh, you don't have to do that. Really, I'll call Abby." OMG! I'm stammering again.

"It's not a problem." He lifts his hands. "I promise not to abduct you or be creepy or anything." He smiles in that disarming, relaxed way. "Text your aunt and tell her your non-stalker friend is going to bring you home after he buys you dinner." He finishes packing my backpack and slings it over his shoulder. Maybe this gallant chivalry is really his natural personality. Maybe he was serious when he complimented me earlier. How can I resist?

So, I text Aunt Charlotte and follow Easton (incidentally, not a bad view) to his SUV where he opens my door. I didn't know guys actually did that. I thought that was a pop culture myth like killer alligators in the sewer or something. The rain has thankfully stopped, so he doesn't rush as he tosses our bags in and hops behind the wheel, starting the engine and turning on the wipers to clear the windshield.

"Where do you NOT want to eat?" he asks as we pull out of the school parking lot. I look at him and raise my brows.

"Girls never want to pick a restaurant, but I find from my extensive dating experience"—he wiggles his eyebrows and smiles—"that they *will* tell you what they don't want without hesitation. No offense to your gender, but girls want control without making it seem like they do, so while they won't say what they want, they will complain when a guy doesn't figure it out." He nods like he's proud he enlightened me with this fortune-cookie wisdom, and because he just looks too adorable, I laugh, a genuine snort that comes out embarrassingly loud. But he just smiles even bigger, and I feel my cheeks pink up again.

"You've got a great laugh," he says, except now he's not smiling. Those smoldering eyes have a searching, thoughtful look again, and I shiver. I turn away because I think if I don't he'll search out all of my secrets. I might just tell him if I don't watch myself.

Flipping down the vanity mirror, I look at the mess that is my hair. Has it looked this bad all day? I pull out the ponytail holder and run my hands through the slightly tangled loose curls. This rainy weather seems to make it less manageable than usual. I try to finger-comb some of the tangles.

"Well, since I have no dating experience—with girls or boys—I can't really argue with that logic." I smile at him, and he's glancing between me and the road, his hands loose on the wheel.

"Your hair looks pretty down like that." His blue-green eyes are as soft as his smile.

My heart flutters, actually flutters. He is probably so playing me right now. He just admitted to having a lot of experience with girls, but I don't care, not one itty bitty bit. Complements from guys, especially guys like Easton Garrett, are rare for me, nonexistent really.

"Thanks." Even though I know I'm blushing for the gazillionth time since meeting him, I force myself to hold his gaze. I don't want Easton to see me as some bashful, simpering girl. Unless I'm totally dense, I think maybe he might like me a little, and I definitely might like him, too. I'm pretty sure I'll let him take me anywhere he wants to go. I wish Abby could see me, us, right now. I think she'd be proud of me and positively green with envy. I make a mental note to call her ASAP and tell her.

*   *   *

After a meal of chicken sandwiches and vanilla shakes, we pull up to my house. Aunt Charlotte's car isn't in the usual spot even though it's almost 6:30.

I'm surprised when Easton shuts off the engine. He gets out and crosses to my side where he opens the door. He gives a small half-bow, sweeping his arm back while I get out of the vehicle. Before closing the door, he reaches in and grabs my bag which he insists on carrying for me, and my heart skips again.

A light rain is falling by now, so we hurry to the covered porch. I reach up, straining on my tiptoes, to grab the key hidden behind a hanging planter attached to the wall near the front door. Not smart for two single females to keep a key hidden right by the door, but hey, we're in the middle of nowhere.

"Sure hope you're serious about not being a stalker." I smile at him as I hold up the key.

"I might just change my mind; you should probably find a better hiding spot." His voice is delicious.

If this were a movie, he'd do one of two things right now. He'd either whip out a knife and go slasher, or he would tell me he can't resist me and sweep me into a passionate kiss while the rain falls around the darkened porch. I'm seriously hoping for scene number two.

But neither occurs. Using the key, I open the door, and I'm thinking this is going to be very anticlimactic when he reaches across me to drop my bag inside of the house. As his arm brushes my stomach, I inhale sharply. His heated gaze locks on me when he straightens. My whole body is tingling, and there is no way he's not feeling it. It's so strong I'm amazed I can't see the charge sparking when I peek down between us.

He's standing close, and I can smell his yummy cologne. It's musky but sweet and reminds me of early-summer nights spent eating ice cream in our porch swing while fireflies twinkle in the yard. It's not overwhelming. He doesn't smell like he took a bath in it; it's just enough.

"Vivian, I know we just met and all, and this sounds like a bad pick-up line, but every time we touch each other, it's like..." But he doesn't finish because Aunt Charlotte's car rattles up the driveway, sputtering to a stop on the other side of the house. Crap! We might have been about to have that movie moment after all (the non-killer one, I mean).

He smiles. "Guess that's your aunt. I should probably meet her, so you can assure her I'm a great guy later when you tell her all about me." There's that lop-sided smile I like so much. He approaches the steps as Aunt Charlotte, school bag in her hand, walks onto the porch. He shakes her hand while he introduces himself as my new after-school hobby, at least until his grades improve.

"Easton was nice enough to bring me home," I interject smiling nervously.

"I guessed that much, Vivian." Aunt Charlotte quirks her lips up in a grin that tells me she knows she interrupted something. Her khakis and shirt are wrinkled and frumpy after spending all day wrangling kindergartners, and her red hair has curled up like mine does with the rainy weather.

Easton must understand that look too because his cheeks flush pink, and he says, "I'll see you tomorrow, Vivian. Thanks again for your help. It was nice to meet you, Charlotte." He gives a short wave, gets back in his SUV, and drives away.

Aunt Charlotte raises one eyebrow. "New 'hobby,' huh?"

I shake my head. "You have no idea."

CHAPTER ELEVEN

FOUR DAYS OF HEAVEN. That's the only way to describe it. Since Tuesday I've spent over an hour every afternoon tutoring Easton, and it has been amazing. He has taken me home after each session, and he even ate supper with Aunt Charlotte and me last night. He complimented her lasagna like it was the best he'd ever had, and I thought Aunt Charlotte's face was going to crack from the size of her permagrin. He hasn't asked me out, but I'm hoping he will soon.

Abby in her sunny-yellow sweat suit corners me while I'm walking to the library and whines, "You have to tutor today? V, it's Friday afternoon. I thought you might want to come over, maybe spend the night." After I first told her about Easton, she was just as excited as I had been, but as the week's gone on, her excitement as waned a little, and I think she's beginning to feel left out, like a third wheel. I haven't officially introduced them yet, and I'm hoping after I do, she'll get over her jealousy.

"I can come over after I tutor Easton; Aunt Charlotte is walking in a charity fund raiser out of town tomorrow, and she's leaving with her friends right after school today. She'll be gone overnight, so I thought you could stay with me, or if you want, I can stay at your house."

"Oooo, I'll stay with you! It'll be great, just the two of us. I need to get away from the parental units anyway. All this family togetherness is making me wanna puke." She makes a gagging noise, and we laugh as we enter the library doors.

Easton is sitting in a plush chair just inside the entry. He walks over, his hands in the pockets of his cargo pants. The green of his t-shirt brings out the green in his sea-tossed eyes, and he smiles mischievously. I tug uncertainly on the gray, V-neck top I borrowed from Aunt Charlotte's closet this morning in an attempt to accentuate the few assets I have. I've never dressed to impress a guy before. If this keeps up, I'll have to have a new wardrobe.

"Easton, this is Abby Johnson. She's my best friend, but you probably guessed that much already." Although I've loosened up considerably over this week, I still manage to say or do at least one embarrassing thing a day in front of him. Yesterday, I was looking at his bicep, and I thought I would die when he had to repeat my name to pull my attention to his face.

He nods, smiles, and reaches out to shake her hand. "Nice to meet you, Abby. Vivian, I have an idea." His eyes are twinkling like a little boy's. "Why don't we call it a week and do something fun? *Beowulf* has waited over a thousand years. I figure that essay can wait until Monday. What do you say?" He tilts his head and raises his brows. He looks excited, his eyes all sparkly.

"Well, if you want to, okay sure. But Abby and I were—"

He interrupts me. "Oh, Abby can come, too." I glance at Abby, and I know it goes against every rule in the friendship handbook, but I really want Abby to disappear, make an excuse why she can't go. This outing has 'date' written all over it but not if Abby tags along.

Before I can say or do anything, Easton grabs my backpack and says, "There's a bonfire at the lake tonight. We can all ride together if you want to go." His aqua eyes flit between Abby and me.

Abby surprises me when she claps her hands excitedly. "Yeah, let's go to the party, V! It's just what I need. You can come to my house with me to get my stuff. I'll tell Mom and Dad I'm staying with you, and we'll go back to your house to get ready. Easton can pick us up there."

She's so excited that she's hanging on my arm, jerking my shoulder slightly up and down with each addition to her plan. She's known Easton all of five minutes, and she is muscling in on his idea. I'm a little annoyed, truth be told. I would so not go with her and some guy even if the guy brought it up first. Get a clue, Ab. This is my chance for a first date, a real date and not some junior high group date to the mall or something. Still, blowing Abby off would do nothing to ease her jealousy, so…

"How 'bout it, Vivian?" Easton gives that lop-sided grin, and I nod my head in agreement.

"Sounds like a plan. I'll call Aunt Charlotte on the way to your house, Abby." I turn to watch her give a squeal and jump up and down.

"Yay! I'll call Mom and Dad now." She pats her pockets and opens her tiny shoulder bag. "Dang, I left my phone in the bathroom. I'll get it and meet you at my car." She turns for the exit, beaming her anticipation. "This is gonna be great!"

After she leaves, Easton shrugs. "I really wanted to take you to the party alone, but I didn't want to hurt her feelings." He smiles sheepishly. He's so cute and so sweet. I'm beginning to think he might be perfect.

"It's okay." I lie. "I'm glad you invited her, too." I don't want him to think I'm a bad friend or a complete slut just trying to get him alone. (But really, is that such a bad thing to be? Everybody's gotta be something. Just kidding—sort of.)

"I'll walk you to her car," he says, holding open the door for me. The sky that's stayed overcast all week threatens rain, and the night will fall faster tonight because of it. Perfect for a bonfire, I think. I've never actually been to one, but I'm guessing darkness is kind of a prerequisite.

After I step through the door, Easton pauses before going down the front steps and does something he hasn't done before. He reaches over and takes my hand in his. The contact is shocking, literally. A tingle travels through my hand into his; it isn't painful. It's exhilarating, like a gust of crisp autumn air or a cold mist on a July day. We both inhale sharply and study each other's face. He swallows visibly, and I swear I can feel his heartbeat through his hand.

I want to kiss her.

I hear Easton's voice, only he hasn't spoken aloud. I'm somehow hearing his thoughts without touching his face. The only times I've been able to hear thoughts I've been actively trying, touching the person's face and willing the connection. It could be the hand holding, I guess, but whatever has caused it, I feel torn. I want more than anything to know how he feels about me, but listening to his thoughts? That's wrong, right? It would be wrong to use my power to encourage him. I shouldn't move nearer to him since he doesn't know I can hear what he's thinking, right? But curiosity trumps morals every time. Maybe it would be okay to just lean in a little closer...

The rain begins to fall, so he pulls me behind one of the support columns in front of the library. This is it. He's going to kiss me! But then an ugly doubt jumps up in my head. What if I put that suggestion into his head in the first place? What if he doesn't want to kiss me at all, and I'm making him believe that he does? As much as I'd like to claim I don't care and it doesn't bother me, it really does. I like Easton, and I want him to like me, too, more than anything. But I'm not willing to stoop to force to get what I want. I refuse to coerce this boy to like me no matter how hot, how unbelievably scrumptious, he is.

He leans in close, and I can smell his very masculine scent and his spearmint gum. I'm just about to pull away when someone else saves me the trouble.

Trista Parmer and Darcy Fletcher step up to the library entrance.

"Hey, Easton." Trista's honey-sweet voice drips toward us from three feet away.

Easton jumps slightly and pulls back from me. The movement is so sudden that I wonder if he's ashamed to be caught about to kiss the outcast or if he woke up from the suggestion I MIGHT have put into his brain.

"Hi, Trista, Darcy." He nods to them and clears his throat.

"Going to the party tonight?" Trista glides closer, looking as though someone poured her into her red jeans and black sweater. I'm reminded of a black widow trapping a fly in its web as she licks her shiny lips. One hand holds the strap of her $300 purse while the other toys with the end of her braid, drawing his eyes to where it rests on her chest.

"Yeah, Vivian, Abby, and I are riding together." When he looks at me, he squeezes the hand he's still holding then laces his fingers even more securely with mine. Could be I didn't brain-jack him after all. My heart flutters hopefully.

Trista doesn't miss the gesture, and her look shoots venom in my direction, I now understand exactly how the poor fly feels.

She flicks her gaze to Darcy who wears a saccharine smile and flips her straight, brunette hair over her shoulder. I don't have to read their minds to know they will never take this offense lightly.

Trista steps close to Easton and brushes her fingers through the slightly shaggy, onyx hair above his ear. He flinches, and I almost laugh out loud. Her shoulders stiffen, and her face carries an ugly scowl at his unspoken rebuff. She recovers quickly, resituating her doe-eyed look from a minute ago. She stands on tiptoe and lightly grasps Easton's shoulder for balance. She rubs her considerable assets on his chest and whispers loudly enough for us all to hear.

"Maybe we can," — she pauses to smile and giggle flirtatiously — "*talk* later tonight when you're alone." Her voice is full of indecent promises. The entire time she has maintained eye contact with me, and I know this display is for my benefit. Oh, I'm sure she wants him. How could she not? But once she saw us together, it became something more. Her hatred of me could never allow this affront to her authority, and she'll stop at nothing to get him and to punish me, but this revelation makes me smile. Not this time, Trista.

As she steps back and continues to glare at me, a surge of electrical power pulses through me, warming my hand. I don't have to look down to know it's glowing. I hide my hand slightly behind my leg but continue to let the force flow into it, into me. This is the first surge I've felt since the cafeteria when I'd pointed Easton out to Abby. It's strange but familiar, like coming home after a long trip.

The falling rain and a broken gutter have managed to wet the concrete steps of the library entrance, and I see a splendid opportunity to test some of those science rules I've had crammed in my head for all these years of high school. My smile becomes as slippery as those steps as I narrow my eyes at her.

Trista gives a little wave, and she and Darcy turn to walk down the steps leading to the sidewalk.

"Watch the steps, girls. They might be slick with all this rain," I warn as, hand still behind my back, I send a small current arcing to the wet concrete.

Trista turns to sneer at me, and just before they step down to the first step, the current races along the water and hits their feet. They fall in a squealing heap down the remaining three steps. Darcy, flopped up to show off her pink thong, lands atop Trista who grunts and propels her off in a huff. She stumbles clumsily to her feet. The sky chooses that instant to let loose a flood — the rain gods must be as amused as I am.

Easton, ever the gentleman, releases my hand and rushes to help Trista and Darcy, who now resemble wet dogs, really ugly wet dogs. Makeup streaks down their cheeks; wet hair sags as little rivulets of water stream over their much too expensive and probably ruined cashmere sweaters. AH, life is good! My inner child runs in a circle, arms raised in triumph.

As Easton reaches them, Trista is dragging Darcy to her feet, yanking down Darcy's sodden skirt.

"Are you okay?" Easton asks, picking up Trista's purse from the bottom step. She doesn't even glance at him because she's too busy burning holes into me with her hate-filled eyes even though there is no way she could know I'd caused her fall. By virtue of witnessing the humiliation though, I've become the reason for it. Since Easton has his back to me, I give her my best bitch smirk and flip a middle-finger salute with the hand I've willed to stop glowing. She purses her lips, flares her nostrils, and radiates fury. Ever the actress though, she sweetens her expression and turns to Easton.

"I'll see you later, Easton." With that she limps away, dragging Darcy behind her.

Trying to wipe the grin from my face, I drop my gaze, pull my phone from my pocket, and pretend to check my messages. After all, I don't want Easton to know how much I *really* enjoyed that.

I'm shocked (no pun intended) at how easily I controlled my powers that time. I knew exactly what to do and how much force to use. I was also able to turn it off just as quickly. Hopefully, none of them saw the thin, blue current leap from my hand to the concrete.

My phone rings; it's Abby.

"Where are you? I'm waiting at the car." I can hear the excitement in her voice.

"Sorry, I'll be right there." Wait till I tell about seeing those two asses-up on the sidewalk! She'll be as giddy as I am. I hang up as Easton approaches me. The rain has slowed to a drizzle when we step down and head toward Abby's car.

"I'm excited about taking you to the party," Easton, about a foot taller than I am, smiles down at me. "I think it will be fun."

"Oh"—I look up, chuckling at the memory of a soggy, pissed off Trista—"I have *no* doubt it's going to be very eventful."

CHAPTER TWELVE

"ABBY, I'M NOT COMFORTABLE in this, and I'll freeze when it gets dark."

"Duh, that's the point, Viv. Easton will have to keep you warm. He'll give you his jacket, or if you're lucky, he won't have a jacket, and he'll, like, have to snuggle you close."

I adjust the tight, lavender blouse that I forgot I even had in my closet. Aunt Charlotte bought it for me last Christmas, but it is way too slinky for me. The gauzy, soft material clings to my body in a way I typically avoid, and the neckline is too low to wear to school without a camisole; however, when Abby pulled the top and cami from the closet, she quickly tossed the undershirt, opting for a pushup bra—also an unworn gift from Aunt Charlotte—instead. With the low-rise jeans she's chosen, I have to admit, I look pretty good. Possibly a little trashy, but what the hell! I deserve a good time.

I decide it would be better to work with Mother Nature tonight and let my hair curl naturally. Abby is just finishing my mini make-over with some light makeup when Easton pulls up.

We slide on our shoes, grab our phones, and laugh all the way out the door to Easton's SUV. Abby, wearing her cutest long-sleeved, pink top, jumps in the back while I climb in the passenger seat before he has a chance to get out and open my door. Ab starts clapping.

"I love this song," she says before she begins singing along to the radio. After I buckle my seatbelt, I look over at Easton. His eyebrows are raised, and his mouth is slightly open. Good! That's just the reaction I was hoping to achieve, and inwardly, I'm doing the happy dance.

"Hey," I say.

"You look… phenomenal." He finally smiles.

"Thanks, so do you," and he really does. His black t-shirt stretches tight across his chest as he turns back to the wheel and slides his palm quickly down the thigh of his dark jeans as though he is wiping away the moisture there. He must be nervous; nervous is good—very good. His messy, midnight hair and blue-green eyes are definitely making *me* sweat.

Abby stops singing. "She does, doesn't she? I told her she would be pretty if she'd just try a little. Don't her boobs look great?" OMG, I wonder if I can crawl under the seat.

"I can't believe you just said that." I cover my face, which I am sure is fire engine red, with my hand and shake my head.

Easton says, "Actually, yeah, they do." He clears his throat in an embarrassed way like he can't believe he just responded to her question. When I peek through my fingers, he has turned his head back to the steering wheel, and his face is as pink as Abby's shirt.

Abby leans between the seats and pokes my shoulder, laughing wickedly.

* * *

As darkness falls we pull up to the lake where a bonfire glows on the rocky shore. Easton opens both doors, and we all walk toward the kids who are gathered around the fire. Some are sitting on logs and rocks with boards across them, creating makeshift benches. Easton nods to some boys, fellow athletes I'm guessing, and Abby and I sit as we are approached by some huge kid I recognize from the cafeteria and hall.

"Hey, man," Easton says performing some overly complicated handshake of fist taps and slaps. Must be a guy thing.

"Glad you finally showed up. Thought I was gonna have to send out a search party." The enormous blond boy slaps Easton playfully on the shoulder.

"Cut me some slack. I have two good reasons I'm late. Cooper, this is Vivian and her friend Abby," Easton points to us in turn.

"Ladies, this Cooper McNeal." Cooper is the same height as Easton, but his arms are massive. Easton's muscular, but Cooper is a giant, a future pro-wrestler for sure. He's not bad-looking either, blond hair, soft brown eyes, and dimples—heartbreaker material. He has an easy country-boy grin, and he's dressed the part in his flannel shirt, boots, worn jeans, and ragged cap. Abby's eyeing him like he's a filet mignon.

"So, this is Vivian! 'Bout time I got to meet you. I've heard nothin' but Vivian, Vivian, Vivian since Tuesday." He pulls me to my feet and gives me a back-thumping hug. From the corner of my eye, I notice Easton's sporting the same look I had when Abby pointed out my attributes earlier. When I'm able to breathe again, I mentally cheer. He's been talking about me to his friend? Could this night get any better! He complimented me twice, and he's been talking about me!

Cooper releases me, and I immediately fall back to my seat, a little dazed both from the hug and the revelation. Then Cooper turns to Abby and sticks out his hand palm up.

"Abby, nice to meet you." When she puts out her hand, he takes it in his open one and actually kisses it. Seriously corny, but Abby giggles and bats her lashes like some chick in an old black and white movie. She's left her glasses at home, and her blue eyes sparkle in the firelight. Her blonde curls are loose around her shoulders.

Easton and I make eye contact, both very surprised by the behavior of our friends. Cooper is still smiling over Abby's hand when Easton says, "Come on, Romeo; let's get a couple of drinks for them." But Cooper doesn't acknowledge Easton. "Coop!" At that, Cooper jerks his head around.

"Oh yeah, okay, be right back, ladies." But he only has eyes for Abby.

After they leave, she grabs my arm. "Oh wow! He's so big and cute. You think he's cute? I love his accent. Where do you think he's from, Texas maybe?" I zone out as Abby rambles in her typical 'I just met a guy' montage. I'm looking at the faces around the fire when I spot Trista, and I have to admit, she looks great. Damn!

She's literally pulled out the big guns tonight. She's about to pop out of her red, sequined top and skinny jeans. I look down at my chest. No way in this world (or any other for that matter) can I compete with her blonde perfection, and all *that* is walking toward

Easton who's pulling some canned sodas from a big cooler in the back of what I assume is Coop's truck. Even in the dim light, I can see Coop's eyes bulge out as much as Trista's bosom when she saunters up to them.

I focus to see if I can hear what they are saying. I'm supposed to be able to use all of these natural energy waves. Sounds are waves, right? Science was never my strong subject, ironically enough.

When I concentrate on the trio, I feel that familiar tingle in my hand, so I hide it by sticking it under my leg, palm down since I'm not sure if I can technically burn myself. I don't want to explain a hole in my jeans that just happens to be shaped like my hand. The voices are audible but barely, so I decide to go in another direction. Before, I never had this much control over my abilities, but apparently, with use comes control. That makes sense I suppose. Every time you exercise a muscle, it grows stronger and easier to use the next time, not that I would know from experience since I'm not sure I can even remember the last time I exercised.

To make the conversation more legible, I decide to focus on brain energy. Ok, who's it going to be? I would feel completely guilty jumping inside of Easton's brain; plus, I'm not super sure I want to hear what he thinks about Trista's boobs, which to his credit he seems to be trying not to ogle. I just met Coop, and he might be harboring some images of Abby I really can't deal with, so that just leaves the devil herself. I'd rather kiss Manly Jenkins than do this, but here goes. As I zero in on Trista's brain, I begin to hear the conversation clearly along with her unspoken commentary.

"So, Easton, do you like my new shirt?" *Come on, look at my boobs. You know you can't resist.*

"Uh, yeah, I guess, Trista. It's very... sparkly." *You guess?*

"Hey, Trista."

"Coop, think I can have one of those, too?" *Coop's definitely noticed. Maybe I should use him to get to Easton.* "It's so hot out here by the fire." *I'll just make sure you notice, Easton Garrett.*

Is Trista rubbing that wet soda can on her neck? The wood beneath my hand starts to smoke when Easton looks at the can then quickly looks away.

"You wanna take a walk around the lake, Easton" *I've got him now.*

"No, I'm here with Vivian. I'll see you later." And as Easton starts toward me, I pull out of Trista's mind. Yay, chalk one up for team Vivian.

"V, look! There's Dillenger." I look in the direction she's nodding, and Dillenger Wescott's walking toward Trista. She immediately grabs his arm, and they walk toward a dark spot where the light from the fire is blocked by some cars. Since the guys have stopped to talk to their teammates, I decide to listen in again. It never hurts to know what your enemy is up to, and she will definitely be up to no good after being rebuffed twice today. But whether they are too far this time or my reception is blocked by the obstacles between us, I can't really hear Dillenger's responses to the conversation. I can, however, still hear inside of Trista's mind, and the part I hear, though one-sided, is undeniably interesting.

I want to get her, and you're going to help me if you want to be one of us. Do you know her friend? Yeah, the short, fat one—Abby.

Abby? Why's she bringing Abby into this? For that matter, how is she going to use Dillenger? Just then the guys return, and I quickly pull myself away from Trista.

"I hope this is okay. It's all I had." Coop is handing Abby the can.

"No, it's fine. Thanks." She is smiling coyly again, and Easton hands me my soda. I open it and takes a sip. He is watching me, and I feel extremely self-conscious as I glance up at him through my lashes.

"You want to maybe take a walk?" He looks hopeful and anxious.

"Sure. Abby, is it okay with you?" I don't want her to feel like I'm ditching her, but I really want to jump up and follow him.

Before she can respond, Cooper booms out, "I'll keep her company. She'll be just fine." Then he remembers the question is for Abby, and he looks at her sheepishly. "I mean if that's alright."

She drops her gaze and looks up at him. "That sounds great." Just like that Easton and I are dismissed, forgotten, as they look at each other smiling shyly. I hand Abby the soda, and Easton takes my hand. We walk away from the fire, the group gathered there, the music playing from someone's car stereo, and walk toward the darkened water.

CHAPTER THIRTEEN

THE BUTTERFLIES IN MY STOMACH feel like pterodactyls. The cloud-covered moon peeks above the dark lake's surface. We are walking slowly, no destination in mind, and he is swinging our joined hands lightly. The darkness partially obscures his face, but I feel his gaze on me.

"I love this lake," he says as I glance at him. He looks across the still water then over at me. Even though the moonlight is weak, it still creates a sparkle in his eye.

I nod. "It's nice here. Aunt Charlotte and I used to come here on Saturday afternoons when I was little." I remember vividly the summer sun beating down, making the water feel that much cooler. We'd pack a picnic lunch and our lawn chairs and buy some cheap water toys that would always leak air and go flat by the end of the day. The smell of sunscreen and plastic beach balls and Aunt Charlotte's laughter when I'd flounder to get on an air mattress, flipping it end over end—some of the happiest days of my life.

"In my hometown there is a lake like this one. Not too big or too small, surrounded by woods." He points toward the dark trees. In the distance, I see lightning flash.

"Guess the storms from today aren't over yet," he says. "That's okay, though; I like those, too."

"I kinda have a fondness for storms, myself," I say, which is true, probably not for the same reasons. The lightning makes me feel alive. I can feel it coming before the weather man has a clue, and the anticipation is like Christmas morning. But I can't really tell him that; I'm too scared he'll run away screaming.

"Hey, did I tell you I got a 100% on all of the make-up work so far?" His smile is almost luminescent.

"Mrs. Crafton told me. She's pretty proud of you." I kick at the pebbled shore.

"Guess you might not be stuck with me for long." The way he says it makes me think he's disappointed.

"Oh, I don't mind being stuck with you. I'm not tired of you yet." I stop walking, and we face each other.

"Good, because you're going to have a hard time getting rid of me." He leans in closer. Just then the sky opens up, and rain sheets down on us.

"Come on!" He runs, pulling me behind him, and by the time we reach the grove of trees to our right, we are both laughing and drenched. The tree branches are thick here, and the early spring leaves shield us from most of the downpour.

Shaking water from his hair and still laughing, he says, "We just can't seem to catch a break."

Before I can respond, he pulls me into his arms. We aren't laughing as he tightens his hold and looks down into my eyes. I wrap my arms around his neck, and he reaches one hand up to wipe a raindrop from my forehead then he drops his hand to my cheek. Cupping my face, he closes his eyes and lightly brushes his lips across mine.

He steps forward, pushing me gently backward toward a tree. Before we reach the tree, he takes his hand from my face and braces it against the tree to cushion my head. I close my eyes and just feel the sensation of his soft lips as he kisses my cheek, the tip of my nose, my forehead.

When he returns to my mouth, he kisses me in earnest, a real boy-girl kiss, like those Aunt Charlotte used to fast forward past on the rented movies we watched when I was younger. My heart is hammering, but so is his. I can feel it pressed against my chest.

I've never been kissed before, but if all kisses are like this, I can't understand why people aren't kissing every minute of the day. This is nothing like I thought it would be. It's better.

Even though I don't know what I'm doing, I kiss him back. I must be doing it right because he makes a groaning sound in his throat that echoes into me. My hands move involuntarily to his head, and I grip his hair. When we finally break apart, we are both breathless, and he takes a step back. If he hadn't kept his arm around my waist, I'm certain I would have fallen. It's cliché and stupid, but I'm light-headed by his nearness, and my pulse is thumping like the beat of a rap song. And there's the spark. It sizzles through me. My whole body is humming with sensation, and I swear tiny azure currents spark between us like static in a fuzzy blanket.

His brows are drawn, and his forehead is crinkled as he looks down into my eyes. Then I register how clearly I can see his face. Minutes before his face had been shadowed, and though the rain has stopped, the dark shelter of the trees should be blocking the weak moonlight. So that must mean...

"Vivian, your eyes. They're glowing."

CHAPTER FOURTEEN

I TRY TO CALM my raging emotions and make the light disappear. I had been so cocky earlier, thinking I had control over my power! I guess my emotions are just too strong because of that kiss. I squeeze them shut then open them quickly, praying that I've hit the 'off' button, but no such luck. The glow is still there. I drop my gaze and my arms, but he doesn't release me and run away as I'm afraid he will.

"I knew it. There's something special about you."

"That's an understatement," I mutter, but at least he didn't say there is something 'wrong' with me. He puts his hand under my chin and forces me to meet his eyes.

"Tell me." There is no anger or fear in his voice.

"I... I... can't, not right now, Easton. I don't even know what to say or how to explain, and I don't want to tonight. I'll tell you but please not now. Let me have this one perfect, amazing moment." I run my hands through my wet hair.

He is silently staring, and I will him to speak even though I'm scared of what he'll say. But he doesn't say anything. Shock registers as he closes his eyes and sweeps his lips across mine again.

I flatten both palms to his chest, and after another long, amazing kiss, he pulls back. When he looks at my hands and sees that my right palm is radiating blue, he takes it in his own larger one and turns it over. The jagged line streaks down my palm. He traces it with his fingers, and it shines even brighter, an intense cobalt.

"Viv, where are you?" Abby's voice comes from nearby. I can vaguely hear her talking to someone, and when I hear a drawling response, I realize it's Cooper.

"They're here somewhere," he says. I see a flashlight beam and wonder how long we've been gone if they're looking for us. Easton closes his hand over mine.

"Guess we have to go," he whispers.

"Are you completely freaked out by all this?" I wave my hand to indicate my eyes and my palm.

"Not at all, Vivian. I knew there was something different about you, about us." Now he waves his hand, the one still holding mine. "Do you think I didn't feel it that first day when I touched you in Crafton's room?" I tilt my head questioningly and open my mouth to reply.

"That was no ordinary shock," he continues before I can reply. "I deliberately touched you in the library when I gave you my pen during our first tutoring session. I wanted to see if it would happen again." I'm speechless, shocking I know, but occasionally it does happen.

He laughs. "You aren't like anyone I've ever met, and I don't mean just this." He runs his thumb over my right eyebrow, meaning my glow-in-the-dark eyes.

We smile at each other.

"Let's go before they call out a search party." He rubs his cheek against mine. "Do you need a minute to, uh…" He trails off motioning with his chin to my eyes.

I close them, take several deep breaths, and sing "Twinkle, Twinkle, Little Star" in my head. It's what I have to do to distract myself whenever I get a shot. Childish, I know, but it worked then, so I figure it's worth a try. Sure enough, it works. When I open them again, they are back to normal.

He gives me a quick peck on the lips and pulls me behind him, still holding my now non-glowing hand.

He smiles, looking back at me. "I'm so happy I suck at English. I think I should thank Mr. Sailers for sending you to me."

He stops and pulls me to him, wiggling his eyebrows up and down. "And I think I'll send Betty Sanders some flowers."

CHAPTER FIFTEEN

EASTON AND I EMERGE from the woods still holding hands. Abby and Coop are nowhere in sight, so we return to what remains of the bonfire. The damp wood only sizzles and smokes as two boys try to get the fire going again. Everyone retreated to their cars during the brief shower, and while most people have ventured back out, a few couples have taken the opportunity to make out, judging by the fogged-up window.

Trista, Darcy, and the rest of the dime squad are gathered around an SUV that probably costs more than my house. The radio is playing, and they're drinking from dark-brown bottles and are clearly drunk or well on their way to being so. As we pass, Trista glances in our direction. She's rubbing herself against a boy I recognize as a football player in an attempt to dance. In her inebriated state, she looks more like she's having some sort of medical emergency than being sexy. She takes in my bedraggled condition and laughs.

"Look at her! She looks like a raccoon with that makeup smeared around her eyes!" Trista laughs, looking to her entourage for them to join in. A couple of the girls follow her example, but the guys don't. One glance at Easton's face, and I see why. His scowl brings his brows closer and makes his nostrils flare a little.

She bends at the waist laughing in a sloppy, intoxicated way, and in a flash forward, I see a middle-aged Trista, face stretched taut from too many plastic surgeries, doing this same thing. It dawns on me that while Trista may seem to have it all, this is it for her. She's living the best years of her life right now with nothing substantial to look forward to, no real path in life except to be some rich man's trophy wife. Eventually, he'll get tired of her, move on to a newer model, and no matter how many enhancements she makes or what trashy outfit she wears, she'll always be this, a caricature of a real human being.

I *should* feel sorry for her. This epiphany *should* take away any affect her ridiculing has on me, and if this were a made-for-TV movie on some women's network, that might happen. But this is real life, and anybody who's ever been plagued by the Trista's of the world will understand. Even if she's pathetic, empty, and probably self-conscious on the inside, I still want to smash her face on the outside. I figure I'd be doing her a favor, making the outside match the inside, lower people's expectations of her; therefore, I would be making her life easier. Hell, I would be a hero! She'd thank me, worship me, exalt me. I would be the center of her little loser world.

An ugly cackle from Darcy brings me out of my brief fantasy and right back to reality.

"Yeah, and look at her hair! Looks like a raccoon's been living in it!" Darcy shrieks and falls all over the poor guy trying to hold her up by the arm.

Easton's grip painfully tightens on my hand, and I look down to see a flash of blue right before he pulls both of our hands behind his back. His eyes tell me not to bother; these bitches aren't worth the effort. I want to zap them so badly, but he's right—for now.

Soon girls, very soon.

I content myself by saying, "Kinda like you two in front of the library." I smile sweetly and turn away, but not before I catch Trista's expression. If looks could kill… Well, looks might not be able to, but I've got a feeling I can. I mentally shake myself. Control, I can hear Aunt Charlotte's voice echoing in my memories from childhood, and taking a deep breath, I chant to myself, "I don't really want to kill Trista. I don't really want to kill Trista." I just want to mess her up really, really bad. I should probably think about anger management classes in the near future before I end up in jail for wiping out Trista and her pack of merry bitches.

Easton pulls me toward what remains of the fire where Abby is standing. The wind has kicked up, in all likelihood bringing more rain. Now that I'm wet and the fire is mostly out, I'm shivering slightly. My flimsy shirt is sticking to me and has become faintly transparent. I cross my arms over my chest and hug myself. Easton rubs my upper arms vigorously.

"I have a blanket in the back of my car. You stay here, and I'll get it. Be right back." He kisses my forehead. I guess Abby was right about not wearing a jacket. As I'm imagining snuggling with Easton under his blanket, Abby grabs my upper arm and whirls me around to face her, her sparkly eyes evidence of her excitement.

"Viv! Where have you been? Wait don't answer that. I think I don't want to know." I give her a devious smile as if to tell her she's missing out on some juicy details.

"I HAVE to tell you something—well, two somethings actually. Cooper asked me out! We're going to the movies tomorrow night. My first real date! Aren't you excited for me? What am I going to wear?" When I open my mouth to respond, she gushes with the rest of her news. "Dillenger talked to me! He, like, just came up and started talking. He asked my name, said he'd seen me in class, and had been too shy to talk to me until now." I try to stop her, but when Abby goes on this way, she's a force of nature, Volcano Abby. You just have to let her gush herself out.

"Dillen, that's what he said to call him, asked for my phone number and said he would text me later."

Okay, to anyone but Abby this whole 'situation' would seem odd. 'Dillen' just up and introduced himself to Abby, a girl who is so far from his usual type she's in a different universe. Abby's great and cute, too, with her purple glasses and blonde curls, but she's not a dime-squad perfect-10. Dillenger is definitely into that kind of girl, gorgeous but shallow. Besides, wasn't he sitting with Darcy in the cafeteria this week?

Then I remember the partial conversation I heard in Trista's head earlier. She'd asked Dillenger if he knew Abby, and I *know* without a doubt that she'd been talking about some kind of revenge on me. It all makes sense. Trista is using Dillenger. She's convinced him to be nice to Abby, but how would that affect me directly? Obviously, any friend wouldn't want to see their BFF played by some fake jerk, and I definitely don't want Abby hurt, but that can't be her only game. She wants me to hurt for taking Easton and just because she hates me so much. Breaking Abby's heart doesn't seem severe enough.

Abby pulls me back to the conversation. "Maybe he'll ask me out, too, hopefully not for tomorrow night. But what if he does? What will I say to Cooper? I don't want to upset him. He's adorable, but Dillen is, like, mouth-watering." She sighs, and I finally see a chance to break into the conversation.

"Abby, let's not borrow trouble. If Dillenger asks you out, you can decide what to do then. So, was he *nice* when he talked to you?"

She rolls her eyes. "Of course he was nice, Vivian! I just told you he asked for my number. Would I give him my number if he wasn't nice?"

I raise one eyebrow.

"Okay, maybe I would, but you aren't getting it! Hello, I'm a desired object now, V. Two boys talked to me in one night! I'm a hot commodity here!" She rubs her hands down her sides and hips and gives a shimmy shake. We both laugh at the same time.

Easton's voice comes from behind me, causing me to jump. "What's so funny?" He's smiling when we turn around. He wraps a soft, green blanket around my shoulders.

Abby's face turns pink, and she sputters before saying, "Uh, we were just discussing… products in demand. Not important," she says, waving her hand and shaking her head to dismiss the conversation.

"Where's Coop anyway?" She hurriedly changes the topic. "The last time I saw him he was going to the truck to get his phone, so he could program in my number. That was twenty minutes ago."

"He's fishing." He shrugs. "Cooper loves fishing. He just can't resist a chance at the big one. Says it's like winning the lottery. You can't win if you don't buy a ticket." I must have looked confused because he grins. "Can't catch a big one if you don't cast a line."

"Oh," I say, raising my chin then nodding.

"I saw him while I was getting the blanket. He asked, no he *told* me to find Abby and ask her to join him by the lake." Easton puts his arm around my waist.

"Ew, like, to fish? I've never been fishing." Abby wrinkles her nose.

"How have you grown up here, lived in this town your whole life, and never fished?" I'm shocked. I guess Ab's more of an indoor girl than I supposed. Maybe, I don't know her as well as I think I do.

She'd implied earlier that she would toss Cooper over for a chance at Dillenger even though any sane person can see what a great guy Cooper is. Easton likes him, so he must be alright. She'd give up a chance with Coop, who clearly adores her, to go out with Dillenger the sleaze. In all fairness, I don't really *know* he's slimy, but he's an associate of Trista's, probably even an accomplice in her plan to get me. Abby is so desperate to be accepted, but would she really do that to Cooper? This is all too much to think about on a Friday night.

I turn to Easton. "Well, this is a great time to teach Abby the fine art of fishing."

"Absolutely," he grins.

We head toward the lakeshore to find Cooper reeling in a small bass as we approach.

"Abby!" he yells, "wanna take it off the hook?"

Her eyes are wide; she tries to smile. "Isn't there someone more qualified for that?" But she does touch the bass with her finger. It immediately flops from the hook where it was suspended and onto the wet ground. Abby squeals, hides behind Cooper, and grabs his shoulders. His loud guffaws make both Easton and me laugh, too.

We fish till midnight, Abby and I sitting on Coop's letterman's jacket. Occasionally, Easton tucks a lock of my damp hair behind my ear or laces his fingers through mine, and I wish we could stay like this forever.

CHAPTER SIXTEEN

I FEEL THE WIND, hear the thunder, see the lightning. I am standing beside my mother. We are waiting for the storm. It is directly above us, loud and severe. My mother is holding out both hands. A small, glowing orb the size of a softball pulses there. It's a smoke and light-filled ball, glowing blue and white. Crackling, powerful lightning branches from the clouds into the sphere.

My eyes are wide as I watch the orb grow brighter and larger. When it is about the size of a basketball, it's so intense that I can't look at it directly. I cover my face and peek through my fingers. The orb's glow reflects onto my mother's face, casting her features in a garish light.

Something behind her catches her attention. She turns her head and casts searching eyes over her shoulder.

They're close. We have to hurry, Vivian.

When she looks at me again, she smiles sadly.

Hold out your hands palms up.

I shake my head.

Don't be scared. It won't hurt you.

I do as I am told. She places the orb, now as large as a car tire, near my palms. It glides to me as though I'm pulling it with a string, like some crazy magic trick.

Her eyes are glowing softly, and my vision begins to tunnel into a brilliant white along the edges.

You'll like your Aunt Charlotte. You've never seen her, but you will soon. I love you, baby. Always remember that.

She slips a note into my front pocket, bends low, and kisses both cheeks. When she straightens, she touches the sphere with the tips of the fingers on her right hand. Her palm glows blue.

* * *

I awake breathless, panting. A light like a thousand candles pushes away the darkness of my room. I feel strange, curiously light. I look down and find myself suspended a few inches above my bed in a huge, pulsing orb, like a giant bubble that radiates heat and energy. Its power glitters iridescent, wickedly beautiful, and I am in the middle of it. Reaching out to touch the side, I notice my hand is glowing with the azure streak. The sphere shimmers with the touch but doesn't go away.

I move my legs, and the energy field moves with me, reshaping around me when I rise to a standing position; the top of the bubble brushes the ceiling. There is no sound, no humming like a power line, no sizzling or crackling, only silence. Because the orb is transparent, I can see my room around me through my tunnel vision. The curtains flutter; some papers from my desk flit near the floor. My still-damp clothes from tonight cling to the edge of the hamper where I threw them when I came home. That's when I remember my guest—Abby.

She is sitting up on the futon where she was sleeping minutes before. Her eyes are enormous, and even from this distance, I can see her trembling. Her hands are covering her mouth as though she is holding in a scream.

"Abby, it's okay." I speak aloud, but if she hears me, she gives no indication. I squeeze my eyes closed and will the bubble away. It slams into my chest the way I imagine a bullet feels; I absorb it into myself, and the force of it flattens me to the bed where I bounce momentarily.

I open my eyes and sling my feet to the floor simultaneously.

"Abby!" But she is gone, her footsteps pounding down the stairs. Swinging around the doorjamb, I take the stairs two at a time. By now I can hear her running through the front door. As I pass the kitchen table, I notice her purse is missing from where she'd tossed it before going with Easton to the party.

When I emerge through the front door, I see her backing her Mustang out of the driveway at breakneck speed. I run out into the yard, the soggy ground squishing underfoot and muddying my too-long pajama bottoms.

"Abby, wait! I can explain!" But can I? I don't even know what happened myself. One minute I'm dreaming about my mom, and the next I'm performing a circus stunt without a net.

What will I say to her anyway? I'm not ready to tell Abby about my gift. If I could get close to her, I could wipe her memory, but that would be twice in a week's time. A week—all of this madness has happened in a week! I've used a power I didn't think I could even control multiple times. I'm not sure how often a mind can be altered without causing damage, and I think I'd be taking a huge chance to wipe poor Abby's mind again in such a short time. I need to talk to Aunt Charlotte, and as the dawn peeks over the top of the house, I go back inside to call her and tell her how badly I've messed up.

* * *

Aunt Charlotte and I are sitting at the kitchen table, a steaming cup of coffee in front of both of us. I've just told her what happened with Abby. It's late Saturday afternoon, and I've called her at least a dozen times, left message after message without success.

"Vivian, this is not your fault. Don't roll your eyes at me. You were dreaming when it happened. How could you possibly have controlled that?" Aunt Charlotte sips and dribbles coffee on her ratty blue t-shirt.

"I know. I know, but now what? Abby won't even talk to me." I take a sip from my mug then lay my head on the table.

"Tell me about the dream again," Aunt Charlotte says calmly as she wipes the spot on her shirt with a napkin but doing absolutely no good.

As I recount the details, I again realize how lucky I am to have Aunt Charlotte. Just sitting here with her, I feel more peaceful. I don't know if it's all her years teaching kindergarten or what, but she is calm incarnate. She nods her head, red curls bouncing as I talk.

When I finish, she says, "The note, the one they found in your pocket. That's how the park rangers knew to contact me. Violet had written my name, address, and number on it. I wish I had it to show you, but they kept it, something about keeping it on file. Vivian, Violet obviously knew or suspected she was about to die. That's why she wrote the note and empowered you." She rubs my head, smoothing back my unruly hair.

"Why haven't we ever talked about this note before now?" I sit up.

"I don't know. I never really thought much about it. I suppose it just seemed like a small detail in the big picture. Violet's death seemed to overshadow everything else." She lays her hands over mine on the table, and I stare at a hole near the collar of her shirt.

"You're right. It is a small detail."

She looks thoughtful. "Maybe the big bubble thing has something to do with the orb in your dream. Maybe it's how you manifest your power or something."

I nod. "I think you're right, and it made me feel completely connected to my mother, but I just *really* wish Abby hadn't witnessed it which brings me back to my question. What am I going to do? Ugh! Aunt Charlotte, why is all of this happening now? All of a sudden I can use and control my powers, and I want to use them. I feel like I'm just beginning to figure out who I am, but at the same time I've totally messed everything up!" I drop my head onto my arms on the table and look up at her.

Aunt Charlotte gives me a sympathetic look. "I don't know, honey. Maybe it's your age. Maybe it's hormones. I don't know, but you'll have to tell her, honey." I open my mouth to argue, but she holds up her hand and continues, "She's your closest friend. She deserves some truth after all these years."

I press my forehead flat on the table, staring at scarred wood, and sigh "You're right. But I have to get her to talk to me first."

CHAPTER SEVENTEEN

MONDAYS SUCK, especially when your best friend still isn't talking to you. Aunt Charlotte gave me a ride to school since Abby won't answer her phone.

I put my books in my locker and grab my lunch; when I slam the door closed, I see Manly Jenkins leaning against the locker next to mine. I tug down the hem of my t-shirt and cross my arms over my chest, lunch bag dangling in my hand.

"So, a 90% on your history project. I received a 95%, top score again." He smirks, and I want to impale him on his ever-present pen collection sticking up like little nerd flags from the front pocket of his striped polo style shirt.

"That's great, Manly." I give a small, half-hearted—make that quarter-hearted—fist pump. I so don't want to deal with his crap today.

"Humph, nice sarcasm, Vivian. Is that your best comeback?" He raises his eyebrows toward side-parted hair.

That's it, asshole. "No, as a matter of fact, it's not." And I lay my glowing palm against the locker near his head and send him a tiny zap. I smile when he jumps and gives a girly squeal. His pens scatter on the hall floor, rolling haphazardly in an escape effort.

"Gotta run, Manly." With that I leave him looking from the locker to me and back again.

I enter the cafeteria late, and Easton meets me at the side door. I haven't spoken to him either except for a short text message

Saturday morning telling me he had to go camping with his family and wouldn't have a cell signal.

"Hey, you," he says, smiling and giving me a little squeeze.

"I tried to find you this morning before school. Abby told me she hadn't seen you and walked away. What's her deal? You two have a fight?"

"Sort of. Let's go sit down, and I'll tell you about it." I grab his hand and head for my usual spot. Abby's not there, of course, and I'm looking around for her when I hear her voice. She's laughing, giggling even, coming through the line with Dillenger Wescott. He's carrying a tray, and she is depositing a bottled water on it. He pays the cashier, and they're walking side-by-side. He leans down occasionally to whisper in her ear, causing her to laugh each time.

When I stop to stare, Easton asks, "What is it?" Then he spots them. "Hm… so that's why she called off her date with Coop."

I remember Abby mentioning a date at the bonfire and her dilemma about Coop. "Guess so." I move again to my table. "We don't have to sit back here if you don't want to. We can sit with your friends if you like." Even though this conversation sounds completely preschool play date, he smiles excitedly.

"Great! I can introduce you to my friends, show you off." He leans in close, lowering his voice on that last part as Dillenger had just done to Abby. "But they better not look too hard, or I'll have to take a suspension because I'm not smart enough to do after school tutoring."

He would fight over me? That's nauseatingly romantic. I love it, but I can't enjoy it. I'm too preoccupied with what's happening with Abby. I try to smile, but it doesn't reach my eyes.

The jock table is two tables to the right of the dime squad table. We have to walk past them to get to our new seats. As I pass, I see Abby sitting in the middle of the pack between Dillenger and Trista who is showing Abby something in her purse. Abby's dressed in her best jeans with sparkling stones on the back pockets and around the top and a designer t-shirt with 'Spoiled' in pink and silver glitter across the front. She's straightened her hair, and she looks more like a stranger than my best friend.

Even though I try not to, I can't help making eye contact with Ab as I walk in front of her. She turns her attention back to Trista but not before I see a look of hurt and even fear in her eyes. It's obvious she realizes I had some control over the energy shield in my room, and I wonder how much she's told them. Probably not much or they would have already crucified me.

When I take my seat beside Easton and across from Cooper, I see Dillenger nudge Abby. He whispers something, and she cups her hand to his ear to respond. He looks at me, smiling cruelly.

* * *

It's been three days. For three days, Abby has avoided me, dodged me, and shunned me. I've tried every day to speak to her, but she's always with Dillenger or Trista. They are deliberately keeping her from me, keeping her from being alone so that I can speak with her.

I've thought a million times about what I'll say when I do get a chance to be alone with her. I'm still not sure what to tell her, but I want to try. When the time comes, I'm hoping it will just pop into my head.

True to his word, Easton hasn't hounded me, probably because I've barely seen him. Baseball practice has started, so he's busy most days after school. Since I've never been athletic, I have zero experience with being part of a team. There may be no 'i' in 'team', but there is absolutely one in 'loneliness', and I'm beginning to be well acquainted with that feeling.

I have no friend and no boyfriend—if that's even what Easton is. We've never formally established a category for our relationship, and while I try to tell myself that's not important to me, it really is. The girl who hates labels needs the security of a label, ironic, huh? I would feel, for lack of a better word, 'normal' if I could say Easton is my boyfriend. The dreaded need for normalcy rears its vindictive head.

I talk to Easton several times a day at school, and he's my ride to and from school with Abby out of the picture, but everyone wants assurance that they are valuable, loved even. And since I've lost Abby, I feel the complete opposite. Aunt Charlotte hasn't been home much either. She's tutoring extra hours. She says she needs money for bills, but I suspect it's to buy me prom stuff, a dress, shoes, all that goes along with that. I told her weeks ago that I didn't plan on going, but I think she assumes I will be now that Easton's in the picture. Secretly, I want to now. In all honesty, I wanted to then, too. But it's easier to pretend indifference when the truth hurts too much to face.

I'm waiting for Easton near the sports complex when I see Trista and Dillenger in workout clothes walking toward Trista's car. Although I feel like a total thumb-sucking coward, I pull back into the shadows, turn on the juice, and listen to their conversation as if I'm standing next to them.

"She is so stupid to think we actually like her." She shakes her head and rolls her eyes.

"Yeah, and when I asked her to prom, I thought she was going to pass out. Good thing she didn't. I could never have picked up her fat ass. As if I would ever be interested in her!" He opens the driver's side of her car and waits as she puts her bag in the backseat.

Trista rounds the front of the red convertible and stands close, very close to him. He grabs her around the waist and tugs her into his arms where she smiles and presses her chest into his.

"But you're SO convincing." She reaches up her hand and runs her fingers through his hair. "She believes it completely, and she has totally cut off that bitch, Vivian." She throws her head back in triumph. "Ha! It's going perfectly, and before you know it, prom will be here. Then this whole 'situation' will be over. No more pretending."

She looks around, checking for witnesses most likely, and kisses him. Not a platonic, 'I heart you' kind of kiss, but an 'I want to rip off your shirt with my teeth,' mouth-scorching kiss.

I'm digging in my bag for my phone, so I can capture this moment on video and send it to Abby when Easton gooses me from behind.

"Hey!" He yells as I jump then and spin to face him. When I whip around again, phone in hand, they are driving away. Frustrated, I comb my fingers through my tangled hair.

So, that's the game—ruin our friendship then dump Abby, leaving her miserably broken. I knew he wasn't sincere, and I should have known Trista was messing around with Dillenger even though when he first came here Darcy was clearly interested in him. She's obviously only using him just as he's using Abby. I'll bet when he's outlived his purpose –after dumping Abby—she'll dump him.

How will I ever convince Abby about Dillenger? I know I probably can't, but I have to try anyway.

I never thought I'd be pissed about being right.

CHAPTER EIGHTEEN

IT'S BEEN TWO WEEKS since Abby spent the night with me. I wish I could say it's better, but I can't. She still ignores me every day at school, and I'm still being blocked by Trista and company every time I try to get close to her.

Easton suggested we do something today since we haven't seen much of each other, so we met up with Cooper at the lake for some sun and fishing. Too bad it hasn't quite gone as planned.

The weather isn't cooperating. As soon as we get to the lake, the wind starts to pick up, and clouds roll in to block the sun, making me shiver occasionally despite my jacket. We still fish most of the afternoon, but evening will be setting in soon. Easton and Cooper are having fun, though. They've caught several good bass which they plan on cooking later.

"We can go to my house as soon as it's dark," Cooper offers while re-baiting his line. "Mom will fry these right up after you clean 'em." He smiles at Easton and nudges him with his shoulder.

Easton, reeling in another fish, protests. "Me? Who says? I've caught more than you, so *you* have to clean them." He holds up his latest catch, a big catfish, which slaps its tail against the rolled cuffs of his long-sleeve, navy shirt.

"We still got an hour or so till dark. I have not yet begun to fight, er, fish." Coop's smiling, casting his line.

"Keep dreamin', man." Easton's dropping the catfish in Cooper's huge cooler turned live well. Their humor's contagious, and I find myself laughing.

He wipes his hands on his ripped jeans and gives me his fishing pole while he takes mine and reels it in to re-bait it for me.

"It's nice to see you smiling, Vivian."

"You don't have to keep doing that you know." I look up at him.

"Doing what? Re-baiting your line? I don't mind. I actually kinda like it." He's looking out across the lake, but he's smiling.

"I enjoy taking care of my girlfriend." I glance up again when he says 'girlfriend.'

"Girlfriend? Hmmmm... do I know her?"

Coop shakes his head, grinning slyly. "I'm just gonna scoot on down here a little. I know when to make my exit." He reels in his line, picks up his chair, and moves down a few hundred yards from us.

Easton lays down the rod and drops to his haunches near my chair so that we are eye level. "You don't want to be my girlfriend?" He squints at me, looks slightly nervous, and begins picking up and tossing the tiny pebbles on the shore.

"I didn't say that. You never *asked* me." I'm only pretending to give him a hard time. I'm really so excited I'm about to burst. In fact, I can feel the tingle in my hand spreading across my whole body.

"So... you want to? Be my girlfriend?" He looks at me, head dropped, through his lashes, and I'm again awed that this gorgeous boy likes me, the outcast.

A huge smile splits my face, and I launch myself at him, wrapping my arms around his neck and knocking him backward. One arm comes around my waist; the other helps stop our tumble. I kiss him quickly all over his face, "Yes, yes, yes!" We are laughing, me still atop him, when two SUVs pull up down the lake from us. Easton either doesn't notice or doesn't care because he raises his head to mine, and we kiss, a long, sweet kiss that leaves me even more tingly.

When he lays his head back on the ground, he looks absolutely serious; his blue-green eyes smolder when I rake my fingers through the hair around his face.

"You're glowing again." But I don't need him to tell me because I can already tell.

"You do this to me. How will we ever make out at the movies?" I'm joking, but deep inside this actually worries me—not the making out thing but controlling my power around him so that others don't notice.

"Guess we'll have to practice making out until you can control it."
He wiggles his eyebrows and grins lopsidedly. I'm about to respond
when I hear a girl's shrill screech. I'd know that wicked-witch laugh
anywhere.

Trista, in a bikini top and shorts, is directing three guys on how
to unload and set up her lounge chair. A bikini in March? Can sili-
cone freeze and explode? I certainly hope so.

As I'm squirming off of Easton, Abby, Darcy, and Dillenger exit
one of the SUVs, and Dillenger grabs a cooler from the back. Once
he sets it down, they all grab glass bottles from inside of it, even
Abby. Abby's drinking with the dime squad? From the way she's
stumbling, she's already had a few.

Easton stands and brushes off his clothes. He says without enthu-
siasm, "We can leave if you want." Down the lake, Coop's making
his way toward us; apparently, he has the same thought.

"No, I'm not running from *any* of them." I pull back my shoulders
and zip my jacket as if that will somehow fortify me for what's to come.

Easton grabs my right hand, pulls me close, and whispers, "Your
eyes." I squeeze them shut. "When are we going to talk about this?"
He's been so patient; I really do owe him an explanation. Opening
my eyes, I shrug and feel super-guilty, but I don't have an answer
for him.

Coop saves me when he walks up, chair and fishing pole in his
hands. "Wanna go?

"Nope, let's fish." I smile, but it doesn't quite reach my eyes.

Coop slaps me on the back and propels me forward slightly.
"Easton, this one's a keeper."

"Yeah, a world record catch I'd say." He puts his arm around my
shoulders, and I punch him playfully in the ribs, giving him a tiny
zap at the same time, for comparing me to a fish.

"Ow!" He rubs his side. "Guess I deserved that."

We're just settling back to our fishing when I feel a strong tug
on my line. "Whoa!" I step back and jerk the line. I tug with all my
force to set the hook while I reel it in. Easton and Cooper are both
shouting their encouragement and advice.

"Keep the line tight!" Coop is all but salivating, jumping around
excitedly like a puppy on a sugar rush.

"Don't let him get away, Vivian!"

"You want me to do it?" Coop asks. Giving him my best irritated look, I jerk the line, wondering if Coop might not have such a bad idea. They will never let me live it down if I lose this fish.

Their voices tumble over each other. "Keep reeling!" "Faster!"

At last the fish emerges close to the bank, and Easton rushes forward to grab it.

"Would you look at that?!" Coop's eyes are big. "That bass has got to be about a seven or eight pounder. Good job, Viv!" He tries to slap me on the back again, but I sidestep his hand and miss most of the force.

Easton's taking it off the hook and admiring it as if it's made of gold instead of scales. "That's an impressive fish. Let's take a picture." He tosses Cooper his phone to capture the moment. My first photo with Easton, and there's a slimy, cold-blooded creature from the deep between us—reminds me of Trista.

"Here, your catch; you hold it." He hands me the bass and stands beside me.

"Say 'I just caught a big fish,' " Coop says, snapping the picture. We come over to admire it, and I am surprised it's actually a good picture. My hair's windblown and crazy, but our smiles jump from screen, and I love it. I'm holding it up again because Easton insists on a shot of just the fish and me to set as the wallpaper on his phone when I see Trista, Dillenger, and Abby approaching us. At least Abby has the decency to look uncomfortable. She's pushing her hair behind her eyes and tugging the hem of her jacket, not daring to make eye contact. But is it because of me or her companions?

Coop drops the fish with the others.

"Doing a little fishing, Easton?" Trista rolls up to Easton and puts her enormous chest on his upper arm as she leans over to examine the photo. He moves slightly to the left to dislodge her from his arm and holds the phone out for her to see.

"Yeah, Vivian just made the biggest catch of the day." He smiles and winks at me as if we're all good friends.

She lifts the sunglasses she's wearing even though it will be dark soon, and the sun hasn't been out all afternoon. She squints, frowning. "Oh! Now I see! The fish is on the *left*!"

Easton and Cooper are tense, their expressions growing cold. But I feel totally relaxed; I raise my eyebrows and sneer. "Trista's got jokes... not very good ones, but I'm sure she's doing her best considering what she's working with, poor thing." I tap my temple to indicate her lack of brains, cross my arms, and look sarcastically sympathetic.

"That's priceless coming from you, loser." She tries to look calm, but the vein popping out in her neck tells me she's fuming. "If it weren't for Easton here"—she lays her hand on his arm—"taking pity on you, you'd be totally invisible now." She looks at him while caressing his arm languidly. "Easton, lover, when's the charity screw over so we can pick up where we left off?" Dillenger laughs drunkenly, and Abby is wide-eyed and speechless. Her colorless face shows shock, and she audibly sucks in a breath.

Easton steps to my right while Coop steps to my left, creating a boy fortress. I vaguely note the sound of thunder and the darkening clouds above us.

"That's enough, Trista," Easton says, his aqua eyes blazing with fury. "There was never any 'we,' despite how hard you threw yourself at me, and this is NOT a 'charity' anything! Vivian and I are together. If you can't accept that, then that's your problem!" He points at her then turns his back to fold our chairs and grab our poles. He's throwing it all in the back of the truck as Coop loads the cooler and dumps the live bait into the lake.

Trista exchanges a malicious look with Dillenger. "Easton, you really should ask Abby about your new girlfriend. After all, who knows a girl better than her ex-best friend?" Abby and I make eye contact then she drops her gaze to her yellow flip flops. I notice then that while Trista's half-naked, Abby's completely covered in her jeans and hoody, just another example of why she'll never be Trista's minion.

Easton ignores her and loads the final chair. Lightning flashes in the distance. Coop's already in his truck. "I'll meet you at my house." He leans out the truck window while he turns the key in the ignition.

"Yeah, we're leaving right now." Easton looks at me and gives a small smile while he takes my hand. Coop drives away as we walk the few steps to Easton's SUV.

Trista's voice is desperate. "Abby, tell them what you told us." She grabs Abby's upper arm and gives a tug.

Strangely, I'm not angry with Abby, only unhappy and hugely disappointed. So much for hoping she'll grow a backbone.

Abby shakes her head, but Dillenger whips her around, eyes narrowed, and looks right in her face. "Do it, Abby!"

They're bullying her, just like always, and she's allowing it to happen. Loud thunder overhead momentarily distracts me. A raindrop plops on my head; the wind loosens my already falling ponytail, but I don't bother tightening it. It will be drenched soon anyway.

Abby's tormentors draw my attention when Dillenger squeezes her wrist hard, the same wrist she hurt in the cafeteria fight. She winces, and I'm taken right back to that pivotal moment weeks ago. The pinprick-tingling rushes through me, arms, legs, torso. I have to hide the glowing, so I quickly drop my eyes. Easton jerks our hands behind our bodies as he steps so close our shoulders touch. I close my eyes and see the growing light bursting in my mind.

"I… I said she did weird stuff. That's all." Abby whimpers as Dillenger tightens his hold.

"And?" Trista pokes Abby in the chest. Abby must have retained some friendship loyalty since she hasn't described everything she saw, or maybe she just doubts her own memory of the event now.

"I said she was a freak." She mumbles the final word and sneaks a quick glance at me, her eyes ashamed and possibly apologetic. Easton makes a disgusted sound and shakes his head. But when he tries to pull me to the passenger side of his SUV, I stand immobile. Abby, the girl who shares my hatred of butter pecan ice cream, the girl who explained to me what a tampon was, the girl who cries every birthday her parents miss, called me a freak.

My hurt morphs to anger. I shake with unreleased rage.

Could I have been right at the bonfire when I thought that I might not know Abby as well I have always believed? How could she say that after all the humiliation we've shared at this girl's hands?

I refuse to believe that she's changed that much in such a short time. We've known each other for too long, been through too much. She will regret all of this; she may already. I scared her in my room, and she reacted—overreacted. Then again, how would I feel if this person I thought I knew suddenly levitated AND hung suspended in a glowing ball-o-light?

Focusing with my eyes still closed, I project into Abby's mind. The sunshine and flowers once so enchantingly perfect are dim and faded, proving my point that she's as unhappy as I am. Her mind reflects her dark mood.

I'm sorry, Abby. I love you, friend.

She jerks her head upright which I feel rather than see, and she's looking at me. The thunder booms.

CHAPTER NINETEEN

"SEE, EASTON, EVEN HER FRIEND thinks she's a freak." Trista's gloating voice pierces into my head like a red-hot poker.

"Thanks, Trista, you've just confirmed I made the right choice." He turns for the SUV. Again, I resist, not on purpose this time; I'm rooted to the spot.

"Are you shaking, freak? Are you afraid?" She steps closer as the rain finally patters lightly on the rocky shore. "Come on, freak. Say something." When I don't respond, she shrieks, "I said say something!"

Then she pushes my shoulder. I take a deep breath, but the energy surges through me. Easton jerks his hand from mine. Rubbing his hand, he lightly pushes Trista away, steps in front of me, and turns my chin up to face him.

"Vivian, look at me." I shake my head, my eyes still closed.

"It's okay." But I know they will see if I do as he says. He turns back at the sound of Trista's laughter.

"I'm not finished with you yet! Better watch yourself." She turns to leave but swings back around. "Oh, and Easton, I was so wrong about you. I misjudged your potential. You're a loser, just like her." She punctuates her taunt by poking her finger into his chest with each word. She flips her hair and walks away. Abby is the last to go.

"V, I… uh…" I open my eyes and look directly into her face. She jumps, gasps, and runs after Trista and Dillenger who drops his arm around her shoulders. I suppose they aren't finished with her yet either.

"Let's go, Vivian." Easton tries to pull me again, but I jerk from his hold. His shocked look hurts me, but I have to get away. With one last look at him, I turn and run through the gathering darkness and the storm.

* * *

I run, blinded by tears and the now pounding rain, with no destination in mind. When I reach the woods, I don't slow down for the branches and twigs that scratch at my face and arms and tug at my hair which has come completely loose and streams behind me.

The lake is fed by a river system with smaller lakes connecting or shooting off from the major river. I follow the river until I reach one of these smaller, secluded lakes. Legs burning and lungs screaming, I stop to rub the stitch begging in my side. I bend, gulping air to feed my starving body. The storm above me reminds me of my dream, fierce and frightening. Thinking of my mother, I can almost hear her voice telling me to hold out my hands.

Standing with my toes at the edge of the lake, I hold out my arms fully extended with palms up. I close my eyes to the pulsing energy. When I open them, an orb glows, radiant in the gloomy night. Lightning forks down into the orb, and it increases in size and strength. With the growing sphere, the lightning and clouds pick up as well, and rain buffets my face and body. The orb swirls with blue and white light, light a crystal ball from an old-school fortune teller but lit from within and buzzing with energy.

When the orb is about four feet across, it blocks the rain. The storm is energizing the orb and me. It pulses, hums, and crackles. The inside of the orb resembles a super-charged static ball where tiny tendrils of current now snake out to touch my hand. It's crazy bright and draws my gaze like a magnet.

My vision tunnels then flashes, and for a minute I'm blinded by a starburst. When my vision returns, everything is tinted electric blue, and I can see energy waves everywhere I look. The natural waves emitted by Earth and sky pulsate in surges depending on the force of the wave. Through the darkness, the life force of animals and fish vibrate nearby, their shapes visible by their energy field. Curvy lines jump with each beat of their hearts.

I turn my head left and right to take it all in, and that's when I see Easton, standing on the edge of the forest, unblinking eyes on me and the orb. He's breathing heavily and staring open mouthed.

Don't be afraid, Easton.

I want to reassure him more, but the lightning calls me back. By now, the sphere engulfs me and shields me from wind and rain. Inside it's warm and peaceful, but to Easton it must look terrifying since the lightning outside is feeding the small blue-white arcs inside that pass effortlessly through me. I spread my arms wide, palms out, and begin to rise out and above the surface of the lake. When I am about twenty feet up, the orb is a ball of pure light, so bright I can no longer see my own body. The severe force empowers me.

My clothes must be burning away. The warmth inside the orb touches my stomach and back. I've never felt this exhilarated. Huge explosions of lightning feed my energy.

When an enormous bolt strikes the sphere, I bend backward taking the full force of it into my chest, into the very core of myself.

My body is drifting back to the ground slowly, while small arcs as gentle as my mother's final touch follow me down. The energy shield doesn't dissolve until my head touches the damp grass then I absorb it just as I had two weeks ago.

As my energy surge settles, I hear my name as if from a great distance. When I open my eyes which still radiate a fading blue light, Easton is kneeling beside me.

CHAPTER TWENTY

I AM LYING ON MY SIDE. My knees are drawn up to my chest, my arms crossed over them, and my entire body feels like lead. Minutes ago, I was unstoppable; now I'm immobile. Easton's speaking, but his voice sounds far away. My vision is slowly returning to normal with only flashes of the energy waves from earlier.

At first, Easton's features are blurred by the pulsing lines, throbbing out like a bull's-eye from his chest and head. As the lines fade and his face appears, his concern is visible in his wrinkled forehead and furrowed brows. He touches my face with his fingertips, standing quickly and unbuttoning his long-sleeve shirt. While he stands over me, I'm once again shielded from the rain which has slowed to a light patter. His shirt is cold and damp against my fevered skin.

"Hold onto me, Vivian."

Trying to nod, my eyes slip closed. He wraps one of my arms around his neck and more firmly secures his shirt to cover me, then he scoops me up with an arm under my bent knees and one under my back.

When my head lolls to his chest, he murmurs, "I've got you. I won't let go."

I am hazily aware of our walk through the forest, but at some point I must have fallen asleep because I awaken tucked safely in the backseat of his SUV with his blanket around me.

"What's your Aunt Charlotte's number?" He pulls his phone from the cup holder in the console. When I don't respond, he speaks loudly. "Vivian, where's your phone? I need to call Charlotte."

My sluggish brain attempts to answer; I remember tossing it into the passenger's seat when I got out earlier to fish. I talked to Aunt Charlotte before we left the house, and she said she'd be with friends all day and would talk to me tonight. Easton's the only other person who ever calls me since Abby's not around, so I put it there rather than keep up with it.

"The... seat," I whisper through a scratchy throat, finding Easton's eyes in the rearview mirror. He parks on the side of the road where the wipers beat time, lulling me to sleep again.

I bounce awake as we pull into my driveway. "Easton?" It's the only word I can manage right now.

"We're at your house. Your Aunt Charlotte's not here. I'm going to take you in and stay with you until she gets home. I just talked to her, and it will be over an hour before she makes it back home. I'm gonna unlock the door then I'll come and get you." Eyelids heavy, I see him unlock the door with the hidden key and return for me. "Where's your room?" he asks after he carries me inside.

"Upstairs." I'm so tired that I feel like I could sleep for a week. My arms and legs don't seem to want to cooperate as I try to tuck myself more closely into his body to make it easier for him to maneuver through the narrow hallway up to my room.

As soon as I am settled atop my bed, pillows piled under my head and shoulders and blankets tucked around me, he disappears back downstairs and returns with a t-shirt which he pulls over his head. It must be his practice shirt because the school logo is spread tightly over his chest.

"What can I do?" He sits on the side of the bed and runs both hands through his wet hair. Before I can answer, he goes to my bathroom and grabs a towel that he uses to carefully dry my hair which is dripping onto the pillows. I suddenly realize how thirsty I am.

"Water, please." My voice croaks.

He leaps into action and returns quickly with a glass of ice water. After I gulp it down, he goes to my bathroom and refills it. The water revives me. As I'm finishing the second glass, he sits again, removes his shoes, props himself beside me, and pulls my head into the comfort of his shoulder.

"So... what... what was that?" His voice rumbles low in his chest and vibrates through me. The shirt he tucked around me is wet and uncomfortable, but I don't want to ruin this moment, so I lie still and try to find a way to explain what I don't even understand myself.

"Easton, I can't believe I'm going to say this, but if you want to leave here and never look back, I'll understand."

"Why would I do that?" He tilts his head so that he can look at my face.

"You have to be completely freaked out by what you just saw." I can't look him in the eye. I don't think I can stand seeing the same expression there as Abby had the night she ran out of my room.

"Yeah, I am, but not so much I'd leave you for it. I *do* think it's time for an explanation, though." He rubs my back as he speaks, and I am so glad he didn't take me up on my offer to leave. Taking a deep breath, I begin to tell the secret I've never told anyone.

"I was born with, uh, talents. My mother had them, and her mother had them, and her mother—as far back as anyone can remember, but apparently, I have more than any of the others." I pull from his embrace to face him for the next part. "I can manipulate energy, the natural energy waves from Earth and from people or animals." I don't actually know if I can control animals, never really needed to know what a dog's thinking, except for Trista, but I guess that doesn't count.

"Just about everything gives off energy of some kind, and I can somehow control it. My mother jump started my powers with lightning right before she died, and, well, everyone else in my family with this power's dead. Since there's no one to ask, I'm not totally sure what happened tonight."

His eyes are serious, but there's no fear in them. "Your Aunt Charlotte, she doesn't do these things?"

"No, just me—aren't I the lucky one?" I drop my head. Suddenly, I feel like the freak. Trista was right. He puts his forehead against mine.

"No, I'm the lucky one." He pulls back and lifts my chin up so that I am looking into his deep-sea eyes. "Vivian, what you did was—what I saw—it was," he says, looking up and shaking his head. He meets my gaze then smiles, "unbelievable, amazing, all that power zapping your body. That explains those feelings I have whenever I'm with you, more alive, like I can do anything. I've felt it from the beginning." He leans far back and takes an assessing look. "So, what can you do? Show me."

"Okay, uh," I look around the room and spot the small lamp I leave on most of the time. Reaching out my glowing palm, I send a miniscule stream of power toward it, making the bulb shine vibrantly. It grows brighter and brighter until the bulb explodes and tiny blue sparks flash before we're in darkness, something I don't mind at all. I just might explode every bulb in town if it keeps Easton sitting here next to me. The only light now comes from my window, but I don't see him jumping up to turn on another light either.

"Pretty cool, huh?" I raise one eyebrow.

"What else?" He's pretending not to be impressed, but his eyes tell me he is. I smile deviously and enter his mind.

I can change memories, alter them.

His wide-eyed stare shows he's undoubtedly impressed now. He opens his mouth but doesn't speak, and his luminous eyes are enormous.

I can listen to your thoughts and put suggestions there.

Quickly realizing how bad this sounds, I amend myself. "Not that I would do that to you or have ever done that to you!" I say this last part aloud while I'm shaking my head vigorously, but then I remember that day in front of the library. "Well, not on purpose anyway."

"What did you get me to do?" He tilts his head, and his brows draw together.

"I'm not, uh, well, uh…"

"Vivian, tell me." He looks a little pissed.

"Okay! I might have made you want to kiss me that day on the library steps." I hurry on. "I accidentally heard you thinking that you wanted to kiss me, and I might have *unintentionally* put that idea in your head." When I finish my bumbling explanation, he smiles roguishly.

"Not unless you put it in there days before, too. I was getting up the courage to kiss you long before then. In fact"—he leans in closer—"I wanted to do that from the second I saw those stormy eyes of yours in Mrs. Crafton's doorway."

I whisper in his head.

I didn't actually have that much guilt over it anyway.

We press our lips together. Holding me tightly, he slides his mouth over mine again and again. Behind my eyelids, the starburst explodes. The lightning must have super-charged me because I easily and effortlessly surround both of us in the energy shield. We float above my bed while he kisses my cheek, my ear, and my neck. When he pulls back, he sees the orb around us and reaches out to touch the side. Unlike the scene he witnessed, this orb doesn't have fury and force; it's comforting, like a blanket fort built on a rainy night.

He drops his hand to my face; his eyelids are half-mast. I pull him close again and put my lips gently on his neck, trailing up to his cheek and back to his mouth.

I love you, Vivian.

I jerk away from him and look him full in the face, but his expression remains as sincere and beautiful as before. He thought it intentionally. He meant for me to overhear it in his mind.

"I love you," he repeats aloud. He'd said it—the "l" word. When Trista had been bad-mouthing me at the lake, he'd stood up to her, but he hadn't used that word, not until now. Do I love him? Oh wow! I really, really want to! But do I?

"I... I..."

"Vivian!" Aunt Charlotte rushes through my bedroom door and bursts my bubble—literally. We drop gracelessly to the bed.

*   *   *

I spend the next hour assuring Aunt Charlotte I'm okay while she counts my fingers and toes, checks me for a concussion, and takes my pulse which is racing after my floating time out with Easton. When she's certain I'm not dying, she gives me the 'I'm very disappointed, young lady' speech.

"Alone in your bedroom with a boy, Vivian?"

Easton is smiling though he's trying to look remorseful by ducking his head. "I'm sorry, Charlotte. I just wanted to make sure she was okay." When Aunt Charlotte purses her lips skeptically, he raises his hands in surrender. "But you are exactly right. I shouldn't have been in her room with her."

The humor of this scene isn't lost on any of us. I have the power to control lightning like some Greek god I learned about in seventh grade language arts. I should, without question, be dead right now, but instead my petite, red-headed, kindergarten-teacher aunt is scolding me for being alone with a hot, hot, hot—Have I mentioned he's hot?—guy!

I giggle but quickly cover my mouth with my hand. Aunt Charlotte's lips quirk in humor, and she turns to leave before she totally ruins her mom moment.

"Vivian, get dressed and come downstairs please," she says walking out. "You"—she points to Easton and crooks her finger motioning him to follow.

He squeezes my hand but replies, "Yes, ma'am," and follows her contritely downstairs.

CHAPTER TWENTY-ONE

I'M FLOATING IN A BALL OF LIGHTNING, looking down at my mother. She isn't looking at me. She's looking back toward the falling tent. I feel strange. My arms and legs tingle. Something has distracted her. No, not some*thing*, some*one*.

They've found us.

Her voice speaks to me while her eyes still search the tree line. I wonder how she knows; then as she turns to me I see shadows moving behind the trees. In the darkness of the storm, all that is clear are the shapes, odd shapes like people hunkered down near the ground. Her gray eyes meet mine, and she smiles softly.

It'll be okay, Vivian. Just keep looking at me.

She rises to me inside her own energy bubble and holds out her hands as she draws close to me. We are together in one large sphere which begins to spin slowly. Lightning cracks wildly around us as the spinning increases in speed. Huge white jags of pure power flash like strobe lights in every direction. In less than a minute, we are moving so quickly that the world outside our orb blurs.

With our heightened speed, the lightning swirls until a funnel of blinding light surrounds our shield. It reaches into the lake, electrifying the water where white-bellied fish float instantly to the surface. The tingling is painful now, and I look down at my body, only it's not all there. My feet and legs are oddly transparent, there but not there.

Don't be afraid. The feeling will be gone in a minute. Squeeze your eyes shut. Don't open them until you feel your feet touch the ground. Then stay hidden until morning. Someone will come for you.

Her own body glows vividly and tiny pinholes of light burst through until her body is nonexistent. Only her essence still exists inside my head.

I have to go now, but someday we'll see each other again. Now, Vivian! Close them now!

I do as she has told me and squeeze my eyes shut. My body slams hard against the ground. When I open my eyes, pine trees soar above me into the raining sky. The noise is deafening now that I am out of the shield.

Turning over onto my belly, I see the lightning tornado where white light arcs in every direction from the whirling vortex. In slow motion the spinning stops, and an explosion shakes the ground. I cower, arms over my head. When I lift my head, I see several bodies scattered all around the forest edge where our car sits. Only one is moving; the rest lie prone on their backs as though they'd been facing the explosion.

I shrink behind an enormous tree. One man staggers to his feet. Blood oozes from a gaping wound in his chest and trickles from his mouth. I can hear his labored breathing as he reaches toward a radio strapped to another man's body.

Most of his features are smeared with blood and dirt and obscured by rain, but his eyes I see clearly. There are no pupils, no irises, and no whites. Shining like wet marbles, they are black, empty, and soulless.

I'm afraid, so afraid of those eyes. Where's my mother? Tears slip down my heated cheeks. She isn't by the river. She's gone. I scream, and a tree near the black-eyed man explodes, leaving a gash on his forehead near his left eye, and knocking him again to the ground where he stays.

*   *   *

"It's okay, Vivian. It's only a dream." Aunt Charlotte is holding me, rocking gently. I clutch her arms even though I am probably bruising her. My heart gallops, and my breathing is harsh. My eyes are open, but at first I see only the empty eyes.

"Shh, stop screaming, Vivian."

Screaming? Then I hear the sound, broken only when I try to suck in air. "She killed herself. She died to save me." The sobs are uncontrollable and loud.

"It was just a dream. It's alright." Aunt Charlotte continues to soothe me.

I pull away. "No! It was real. This was a memory not a dream, Aunt Charlotte. She created this... this thing that looked like a tornado but was made of lightning. It swirled around and around us until I just" —I pause not really knowing what I had done—"disappeared. I woke up in the forest away from the light, but I could still see it—her—until it exploded."

Aunt Charlotte is very still. "Go on," she says calmly, only this time I don't share her peace.

"These men were after us, and she killed them all except for one guy. But, Aunt Charlotte, I don't think he was human. He had these black eyes, like" —I struggle for a description—""like marbles or stones."

"Did he see you? This man?" Her brow is wrinkled with concern, and it briefly flashes through my mind that this is a strange question.

"I don't think so. I screamed, and the tree exploded then I woke up." I stare down at the cherry-topped cupcakes on my pajama pants without seeing them. All I can see are those eyes.

"You screamed? I thought Violet was screaming when you exploded the tree."

I look back at her sleep-frizzed hair and white nightgown. "No, it was me, not her. She was already... gone." I bury my head in my hands.

"Vivian, I think you're right. This was a memory coming out." She stands and walks to the window, looking out on the pre-dawn sky.

"Honey, I did some research yesterday." She looks haltingly back at me, unsure how to begin. "That's why I wasn't here when Easton brought you home. I wasn't with friends. I went to the park where you were found then to the local library in town to look through old newspapers."

"Why?" I sniff and grab a tissue from the box beside my bed.

"I wanted to see if the rangers who found you could tell me about it. I've never actually talked to them. They had turned you over to social services when I arrived to pick you up. You have so many questions that I can't answer, and I wanted to learn all I could about Violet's death. These dreams, they have to be important. There *must* be a reason you're reliving it all now. Whether it's because you've been using your powers lately or your age, I don't know, but I want to help you find your answers, fill in the gaps." She is crying now, and I take her a tissue.

"I'm sorry." She gives a nervous laugh. "I should be strong for you, not a blubbering basket case."

"Aunt Charlotte, you are my rock. I couldn't make it without you." I hug her tightly.

"I'm afraid I haven't really done much to help you, though. All the personnel have changed in the state park administration since you were found. In fact, that park is officially closed now. I asked the woman I spoke to for some forwarding information on the two rangers, but…" Her eyes drop from my face.

"What is it? Tell me, please."

Her blue eyes come back to me. "They're missing, Vivian, presumed dead. Shortly after you were discovered, they were part of a search party out to locate some missing hikers. They never returned. Their bodies, their gear, were never located—just poof! Gone."

I turn to walk to my bed where I sit on the edge, sensing that whatever is coming next is bad.

"So, I traveled to the social service office where you were taken after leaving the park. Your records are gone, too. They don't have a file at all. The note from Violet, your paperwork…"

"Poof," I finish for her.

Numbness grips my body when she nods solemnly, and for a minute I can't even think. This is all too coincidental. First, the rangers, then my records? Both gone? The black-stone eyes flash into my mind." The men from my dream, Aunt Charlotte, do you think they have something to do with this?" Her hesitation is my answer. "But how have they not found me? I mean, it's not like we've been living in secret-spy mode here."

She looks at her bare feet. "I changed our names." She hurries on. "I should have told you a long time ago, but I didn't want to scare you. On my drive to pick you up for the first time, I made up my mind. I would change our names—our last names—and move us to some small town in the middle of nowhere. It was my only option.

Violet's last call made my choice clear. She was terrified then she was dead." Her voice breaks, and she sobs but continues. "I had to keep you safe."

Aunt Charlotte moves to sit beside me. "I'm so sorry, honey. Seems like that's all I've said to you lately." Her eyes shine with unshed tears, and her nose resembles a tiny tomato.

"What was it before?"

Aunt Charlotte's brows draw together. "What was what?"

"My name. What was it before?" I know with all the bombs she's just dropped on me, this question sounds stupid, but right now it's all that seems to matter, to connect who I was with who I have become.

A small smile flashes on her face. "Vincent. Vivian Vincent."

Another "v" —I should have known.

CHAPTER TWENTY-TWO

I CAN'T BELIEVE PROM is tomorrow night. I was right about Aunt Charlotte's extra tutoring hours; she surprised me with a shopping trip last week and bought me way more stuff than I wanted, but it made her happy, and we both need a little more of that lately.

The final bell just rang, and I'm gathering all the books I'll need for the weekend even though it's only Thursday. It's an unwritten rule that most of the juniors and seniors won't be at school tomorrow between the hair appointments and all the primping required for this archaic ritual.

It's not that I'm unexcited about the big event. I am, really, sort of. I'd just be a whole lot more excited if Abby and I were getting ready together. I never thought I'd miss her rambling and giddiness so much. We haven't spoken since that day at the lake three weeks ago. She's still trailing around behind Trista and Dillenger. Every time I see them all at lunch, I miss Ab a little more, and I've caught her secretly glancing my way a few times, so maybe she misses me, too.

As I'm making my way to the sports complex to meet Easton, I hear someone call my name and turn to see Abby waving at me to stop. Trista's car is already gone from its usual spot in the front row.

"Viv, wait up." Abby's panting slightly from her short jog across the parking lot, and as she gets closer, I can see she's put on a little weight, not much but enough to make her cheeks rounder. Abby's a stress-eater, always has been. When her parents were thinking about moving to the city last summer to be closer to their jobs, Abby put on about fifteen pounds before they finally decided to give up that idea.

"Hey," I say so unenthusiastically that she drops her gaze to the asphalt.

"Listen, V, I don't really know how to say this, and I'm not sure it will mean anything anyway, but I'm sorry for all this." She glances up and motions around with her hands as though the last few weeks are playing out around us. "And for what it's worth, I've really missed you."

I don't know how to respond. Is this something Trista put her up to? Is it all part of her master plan? It's pretty convenient that she's already gone for the day.

"Trista know you're talking to me? You might get a spanking for disobeying her, ya know?" The sarcasm just slips out unintentionally, and Abby looks hurt. Maybe she is being sincere after all.

"Guess I deserve that, and yes, she does know. In fact, she wanted me to pretend to apologize to you, to get you to sit next to me at prom. They have something planned for you, but I don't know what it is because I'm not part of the dime squad." She drops her head, and picks at nonexistent fuzz on her pink t-shirt. When she lifts her head again, tears are sliding down her cheeks.

"Ab," I begin, but she stops me.

"It's okay. I know I'm not one of them, never will be. Dillenger couldn't possibly want someone like me, but I was just so hurt and angry with you. I felt betrayed. It's obvious you aren't telling me something important. I've been doing a lot of thinking, remembering. There have been other weird things over the years, huh? Things I never really thought about till now." Her head is tilted, and her eyes are narrowed.

Taking a deep breath, I nod slowly. "Yeah, Abby, there have. I should have told you before now, but Aunt Charlotte was the only person who knew. I'm incredibly sorry I didn't tell you." Her face brightens into a real smile at my apology, and just like that, she's Abby again, my Abby.

"Oh, V! I've missed you!" She grabs me in a bear hug.

"Me, too, but you're squashing me, Ab," I manage to squeeze out in a tiny voice.

She releases me but keeps her arm around my shoulder. "Come on," she says with a smile that shows off all of her sparkly white teeth, "we have *so* much to talk about."

*   *   *

Abby takes me home for the first time in nearly a month. Easton follows, and Aunt Charlotte cooks an enormous meal. We all have a long talk, and I enlighten Abby just as I did Easton after my mid-air escapade. Telling it the second time is easier, and Abby sits in open-mouth silence until I finish then she nods, asks me if I can brainjack her math teacher into changing her grade, and pops another mouthful of spaghetti into her mouth. It's as if the last few weeks have never happened. Before dessert, she's filling me in on all the latest gossip and rambling happily about her prom dress. Finally, cheesecake eaten and dishes washed, we move to the front porch. Easton and I sit in the porch swing, and Abby sits on the top step where she lies back flat on the porch.

"So what are we gonna do about prom?" Abby is licking a cherry lollipop she pulled from the stash in her purse.

"We aren't going to do anything." I take Easton's hand in mine and swing my feet to make the porch swing rock.

"What do you mean?" Easton selects a grape lollipop from Abby's collection.

"Trista and her goons have something planned for me, us"—I point to him—"for tomorrow night."

"I don't know what, but I'm supposed to be pretending to get back in good with you two to lure you into the trap." Abby waves her hand with a mock sinister look.

"Are you?" Easton gives Abby a serious stare.

"No, Easton, I'm not." But she has an odd look on her face, and I get a sick feeling in the pit of my stomach.

CHAPTER TWENTY-THREE

"SWEETIE, YOU LOOK AMAZING." Aunt Charlotte has posed me on every available surface and has snapped photo after photo.

"We've just spent the last six hours getting me ready, Aunt Charlotte, so I sure hope so."

Aunt Charlotte took the entire day off from school, and after sleeping in, we ate a lunch of Belgian waffles. Then she curled my hair and piled it loosely atop my head with about a thousand pins and hair clips, applied a full coat of makeup, and helped me slink into my dress, a form-fitting number with a slit up the side that reaches my thigh and a plunging neckline. It's a shimmering silver-white material that sparkles like diamonds and matches fantastically with my new strappy silver heels. I feel exactly like a 1940s starlit—if that starlit were a tad self-conscious showing so much cleavage.

"Aunt Charlotte, I'm still kinda shocked you're letting me wear this dress." I give a small, rearranging tug on the scant material between my boobs. She bats my hands away.

"Stop pulling at it, Vivian. You have a rockin' body. You should show it off."

I roll my eyes. "First of all, ew. Hearing you say that is a trifle disturbing. Second, I don't think anybody uses 'rockin' anymore, and third, aren't you supposed to be warning me about drinking and letting Easton take advantage of me on prom night? Boys and beer are evil and all that?"

Aunt Charlotte doesn't miss a beat. She just smirks and goes to her purse on the couch.

"As a matter of fact, I have something else for you. Honey, you are almost seventeen and are *way* more mature than I was at your age, AND I do have at least part of that covered." Then she tosses me the small box she's just pulled from her purse. It only takes a peek to register what it is.

"Condoms? OMG, Aunt Charlotte! You bought me condoms?! I am completely embarrassed." I hold the box as though it's a hideous spider readying itself to leap from my palm to my nose.

"Well, I wanted you to be prepared. Mind you I'm not saying I want you to, uh"—she shrugs uncomfortably—"you know, but if you do, I also want you protected. Teen pregnancy rates are astronomical, and Easton's probably a bit more experienced in such things than you are." Pink-cheeked and obviously trying to convince herself as much as me that this plan of hers is a good one, she smiles. "I do not want you bringing home either a baby or a nasty disease."

I'm so traumatized I can't even shake my head. All I can manage are a series of blinks, feeling like I did in freshmen health class when we had to color-code diagrams of the human reproductive system. After I recover, I can't stop the snort of laughter blurting past my lips. *This* is why I love this woman. Placing one hand on my hip, I wag my finger at her.

"First whiskey then rubbers. Aunt Charlotte, I think we need to reevaluate your habits of late." She sniggers, and I hear Easton pulling into the driveway, saving me from further humiliation. I toss the box back to her, eyes wide, telling her without talking that I do not intend to need them anytime soon. But she just shoves them into the shiny silver wrist clutch I'm carrying tonight. I start to protest again, but Easton is walking up the steps.

When he walks in looking like he stepped off the cover of a magazine, I forget to breathe. Even though he is dressed in an ordinary black tux, he looks far from traditional. He's wearing a black tie that's loose at the collar which is unbuttoned, and his cuffs, also unbuttoned, are hanging out of his open jacket. His black hair is slightly spiky and in his usual just-got-out-of-bed style. In his hand is a bouquet of blue orchids, vibrant and electric.

When I finally manage to drag my eyes to his face, he's staring at me, scanning me from head to toe as I've been doing to him.

"You look" —he shakes his head vacantly which makes me smile—"stunning."

"Thank you." I can feel the heat in my cheeks. "So do you." A lame finish, but that's all I can manage. When he still doesn't move, I finally point to the flowers. "Are those for me?"

"Oh, yeah, sorry." He laughs and steps toward me. From the corner of my eye, I see Aunt Charlotte reaching for her camera.

"I know I'm supposed to bring you a corsage, but" —he shrugs— "when I went to the florist's shop, it just didn't feel right."

"They're beautiful, exactly right." I take the flowers to the mirror above the couch, snap a few blossoms off of the stems, and place them gently in my curls. Handing all but one to Aunt Charlotte to put in a vase of water, I return to stand in front of Easton where I place the leftover orchid in the buttonhole of his jacket. He takes both my hands and kisses my cheek.

"Oh, do that again! I want to get a picture." Aunt Charlotte has returned, armed with her camera. We pose for the next ten minutes till my face aches from the smiling before we finally leave.

In his SUV, Easton fidgets with the radio, his seatbelt, his tie. When I can't ignore it any longer, I turn toward him. "Easton, what's wrong? You're obviously nervous."

He sighs. "I just want everything to be perfect tonight. You deserve to have a great prom, and I don't want those assholes to ruin it."

I touch his hand where it rests on the gear shift. "No matter what happens later, this moment right now is perfect."

He grins. "You know we don't have to go. If you want, we can drive right past the gym."

"I'm still not running away. You're sweet, but whatever happens" —my turn to shrug— "happens. Besides, check out this split." I lean over to give him a view of the opening up the leg of my gown. "I'm pretty sure it's high enough that I can still kick Trista's ass."

My unconcerned smile's as fake as Trista's hair extensions. On the inside I'm as anxious as he is, but I'll be damned if I let them see it. I'm not scared, just on edge wondering when and how the punishment will come. I'm also not totally certain if Abby's returned from the dark side. A double-cross would not be good. I'm not entirely sure how I would react to that.

As we pull into a parking spot, Cooper's climbing out of his truck. He hurries over to my door and opens it. Giving a wolf whistle, he holds out his hand to help me out. "Dang, girl! Look at you!" He's wearing a tux, boots, a cowboy hat, and a smile as big as Texas.

Easton walks around to my side and takes my hand from Cooper. He moves between the two of us and puts his arm around my waist. "Hands off, man." But he's grinning lopsidedly, and his aqua eyes are turned up slightly at the corners. "Get your own date."

"I wish. Vivian, when you wanna dance with a real man tonight, you just gimme a holler." Cooper winks and begins walking with us across the parking lot to the open double doors leading into the gym lobby.

We're all temporarily blinded by the darkness of the interior. The gym's decorated with clear twinkle lights and glittery silver stars. A band that probably sounds much better in the lead singer's garage plays from the stage at the far end where the basketball goals have been lifted. The prom committee has gone all out, creating a center ring in the middle of the ceiling from which hundreds of blue and silver streamers dip into graceful swoops. The lights sparkle, and the stars twirl lazily, but the smell still reminds me where I am. No matter how much they dress it up, the gym's been saturated with teenage sweat for too long to let anyone forget it's just a gym with tons of overpriced decorations. But it *is* pretty, maybe even a little magical if I squint my eyes and tilt my head.

We find an empty table, and Coop, a couple of other athletes and their dates sit with us. It's actually fun listening to the guys kid each other, and I'm starting to relax when I see Trista and her date, some random senior, come into the gym. Of course, she looks fantastic in a skin-tight, hot pink dress. Unlike mine, it's short, so short there's no way she can bend over without exposing Victoria's secret. Her hair is a blonde waterfall, smooth and shiny.

As I'm watching her stilettos clip across the room, Easton, standing behind me, leans close. "Look." I follow the direction of his gaze and see Abby, smiling broadly, enter close behind Trista. She's wearing a purple dress with a tutu-like bottom. When she turns to talk to someone over her shoulder, my stomach lurches. Dillenger is trailing behind her. He pulls her back, using her to shield him while he sneaks a sip from a black pocket flask. Not even a tux can hide what a jerk he really is.

Like a magnet, Abby zeroes in on me, and our eyes lock before she turns back to him and pulls him through the doorway. What is she doing? Why is she with him? I don't have to break into Easton's thoughts to know he's thinking the same thing because he drops into the chair next to me, puts his arm around my shoulders, and pulls me close to whisper in my ear. "Did you know she was coming with him?"

"No, but I didn't really ask her either." We watch them cross to Trista's table, the largest and nearest the stage. I smile and look at him, again trying to sound carefree. "Dance with me. It's a slow song, so I probably won't embarrass either of us too badly."

After he pulls out my chair, he winks. "I thought you'd never ask."

While I'm trying to keep from stepping on his feet, Abby, purple toile flopping, approaches our table. Cooper jumps up, removes his hat, and the two of them talk in that same teasing manner as the night of the bonfire. Though I can't hear them, they are obviously flirting, judging by how she keeps touching his arms and chest, and I really want to use my power to listen in, but now that Abby knows about my abilities I would feel too guilty about it.

Easton is holding my hand against his chest, and I lay my head on his shoulder. Maybe this night will turn out okay after all. Abby will end up with Cooper, and I will find the perfect time to tell Easton how much I care about him. I still haven't told him I love him, and he hasn't said it again either. I'm afraid my lack of response must have really hurt him, and I want to make it right, but I'm waiting for *that* moment. I figure I'll recognize it when it arrives.

When the song ends, he leads me back to our table, but Abby's gone. Coop's face is scarlet, and he's breathing heavily.

"Coop, what's wrong?" Easton's brows are drawn together, and he immediately tenses, probably because of Trista's threats.

Coop points in Trista's direction where Abby stands, blonde head down, while Trista berates her. Dillenger laughs menacingly as he pulls the flask from his pocket, not even trying to hide it now. Abby swipes a hand under her eyes, and Trista throws up her hands apparently disgusted by Abby and steps away from Abby who nearly runs to the bathroom, trying to escape her. I grab my purse. She may need a little fix-up after her crying, and Aunt Charlotte insisted I bring reinforcements in the form of powder and lip gloss. I refuse to let Trista ruin Abby's night.

"I'll check on her. Be right back."

As I enter the bathroom, I hear crying in the stall at the far end of the room, so I knock softly on the metal stall door. "Abby, open the door."

"Why's she so mean to us?" she asks, opening the stall door then quickly latching it behind me. Since she's picked the handicap-accessible stall, we have no trouble fitting inside. Laying my tiny purse on top of the TP dispenser, I grab some tissue and dab at her face.

"I'd like to believe she's unhappy and insecure, so she tries to make everyone else feel that way, too. However"—I sigh—"I really think she's just a bitch, Ab."

Abby giggles through her tears. "Yeah, that's gotta be it." Then, swiping at her nose, she turns serious again. "She's, like, so… nasty. I tried to tell her to leave you alone and that I'm gonna let Coop take me home, but she started yelling and calling me names." The waterworks start again when she sobs out, "V, I made such a huge mistake with you and with Cooper. How could I dump both of you?"

The outer bathroom door creaks open, and I want to get her out of here, so she's not embarrassed even more by having someone overhear our discussion. "It's okay. Pull it together. We'll ignore her, do our own thing like always. It'll be fine. We'll fix your makeup, or *you* can fix it since I really don't know what I'm doing, and we'll have a great time with Easton and Cooper."

She takes the tissue from me. "Yeah, you're right. Let's go." She sniffs, gives a weak smile, and takes my forearm. When we open the stall door, Trista, Darcy, and three other heavily made up girls are waiting for us, arms crossed. They look like some deranged advertisement for formals.

"Well, well, how nice of you and your streetwalker back-up dancers to check on us." I pull my arm from Abby's grip and stand with my hands perched on my hips.

"Well, well, how predictable for you to come to the aid of your fat friend who just can't make up her mind where she owes her loyalty." She steps closer, practically in my face, her perfectly glossed mouth an ugly sneer. The glitter in her eye shadow twinkles as she narrows her eyes.

Doubt creeps into my mind. I remember Abby saying that Trista wanted her to help with the plan to get me at prom, and for a moment, I doubt Abby's sincerity. Is this all part of the plan? Did Abby lure me in here, so they could trap me, outnumber me?

No, Abby's come back to her senses. She's my friend, right? Glancing at Abby, I see her head is down—not an auspicious sign for the good guys. I don't think I can take a betrayal and a beat down at the same time. Shit! Why can't Trista just crawl back under her rock and leave me alone for one night?

"Abby will always be my friend, and I will always defend her from the bitches of the world, Trista." I narrow my eyes then smirk.

"Really? You think she needs protection from me? Abby's one of *us*, loser. Aren't you, Abby?" She tilts her head to Abby for conformation. Her partners in crime step around Trista, closer to me.

Okay, Abby, now would be a good time to, oh, I don't know, reach down and grab a set. I wait for what seems like an eternity but in reality is only a few seconds. Finally, I turn and face Abby. "Abby?" She won't look at me. This could go extraordinarily bad for me.

Trista finds her chance. She pushes me to the floor where I land hard on my hip. My hand starts to tingle.

Breathe, in through the nose, out through the mouth. This is my prom, and I don't think Aunt Charlotte can get blood out of this dress. I do NOT want to ruin this dress or this night with this same crap as always.

I try to get up, but Trista pushes me back down while her puppets laugh. When I try again, she slaps me across the face. With my head still turned away from her, I reflexively reach up and cover the burning hand print with my own hand. My cheek is fevered and stinging, and I see one perfect blue orchid lying on the scuffed tile floor, knocked from my hair by the force of the slap. As I turn back to her, I tremble and begin to lift my hand to retaliate, consequences be damned, but Abby steps between us, pushing Trista into Darcy and hiding my gleaming palm.

"Leave her alone, Trista!" She knows I'm close to losing it.

"What the hell are you doing?" Trista looks incredulous, her nostrils flared like a Barbie doll nightmare. "You're choosing her?! A loser?! I thought we understood each other. You are a NOTHING without me! Dillenger would never have glanced at you if I hadn't told him to. You're supposed to be helping me!"

"That's a lie! I NEVER agreed to any plan to help you!" Abby turns to me and hauls me to my feet by the upper arms, but she quickly whips back to face our nemesis. My eyes must be glowing, but no one seems to notice. They're all too focused on the drama unfolding between Abby and Trista.

"I'm done with you, Trista. I can't believe I let myself trail around behind you like a dog, licking your feet, eating the scraps you tossed from your precious dime-squad table! I made a fool of myself, and for what? So Dillenger can pretend to like me then make fun of me behind my back? And sometimes not even bothering to wait for me to leave to do that, just saying whatever he wants right in front of me. I'm as pathetic as you are, thinking Easton would ever want you instead of Vivian!"

Whoa, go Abby! It's like a dam has broken. She's jerking her hands and head around, eyes wild and moving closer to the girls who all tower over her short frame. She's like an avenging fairy in all that fluff.

Trista's lips compress so tightly they form a nonexistent line. Her jaw is clenched hard, and I really hope she breaks her teeth. Her eyes are enormous. "You're going to regret this!" She launches herself at Abby and grabs her by her bouncy curls.

Abby squeals, and the other vultures rush in around them, effectively separating me from Abby. I hear Abby scream as her head slams against the metal divider between stalls. I tug and fling the girls, afraid to use my powers for fear of hurting Abby, too. She screams again, and I briefly glimpse her as Trista tosses her to the tile floor inside the stall. When I at last get past Trista's sentinels, I watch as Abby's head whacks against the metal bar on the wall beside the toilet, and she grips her head with both hands.

Cackling, Trista turns to me, and we are nose-to-nose, exactly where I want to be. Abby and the others move out of the way, I forget all logic and let my anger take over. Trista narrows her eyes and bares her teeth. When she slaps her hand next to my head, right on the metal divider, I smile. Perfect.

"Your turn," she says, leaning in toward me.

"My thought exactly." I smack my hand above hers. The energy flows quickly from my chest, through my arm, and out of my hand. The shock I gave Manly was a tickle compared to this one. Her body twitches repeatedly. Her eyes roll crazily while her hair stands on end. She tries to jerk her hand off the divider, but that's impossible until I decide to release her. The joy I get from watching her is exceeded only by the sheer bliss I experience from the look on her face. She looks completely... shocked, literally!

"What is it, Trista? Is something wrong?" I use my most fake-sincere voice, speaking to her as if she's a four-year-old who's fallen on the sidewalk.

When I remove my hand, Trista sprawls to the floor, sliding down the stall wall, and plopping, legs spread, on the floor. Her hair is not quite as smooth or as shiny anymore, and she'll probably smell like burned hair for a week. She's blinking as though that will help her understand what's happened; her palm bears a small black mark where the charge entered. Putting both hands on her cheeks, I shake my head slowly.

"You're kinda hot. I think you might have a fever. You should probably go home right away."

I walk over to Abby and help her to her feet. She's still holds her head with one hand and grabs my forearm with the other. Her smile is huge as we walk past the other gawking, speechless girls, who then rush in to save their beloved leader.

"Ab, you smell something?"

Abby sniffs dramatically, filling her lungs in an exaggerated way.

"Is that chicken?" We burst out laughing at her joke. "It's a little crowded in here, V. We should get outta here."

*   *   *

We're both smiling when we go to collect Easton and Cooper at our table. The other couples are dancing, so they're alone now.

"What happened? You two were gone forever?" Easton stands, holding a glass of punch in his hand. When he notices the bruise and bump on Abby's forehead, he set the glass down abruptly, causing punch to splash over his finger. "What's wrong? Did Trista follow you?" Cooper stands, too, at the urgent sound in Easton's voice.

"We'll tell you about it in the car. We've decided we can have a better time at my house. Oh, maybe we can even go fishing!" Abby jumps excitedly and claps her hands, making her tutu puff out.

I raise my eyebrows at Abby's surprising suggestion, but Cooper lets out a whoop and reaches for her hand to lead her across the dance floor toward the door. I should be worried about using my powers in front of those girls, but I feel like I did after the fight with Betty Sanders. I don't really care. I'll worry about fixing it all later. Right now, I'm as giddy as a kid on Christmas morning. My gift is still laid out on the bathroom floor. Easton's curiosity has drawn his brows together. He tilts his head toward me.

"Let's just say Trista's going to need some serious one-on-one time with her hairdresser." I nudge Abby with my elbow.

"And maybe an electrician," Abby whispers. The two of us burst out laughing at Abby's comment.

I reach for my purse when we start to go and remember with a curse that I left it in the stall where I wiped off Abby's face. I'd just decided to leave it behind when Trista bangs open the bathroom door, looking slightly insane and really pissed off. Her hair's even wilder than before, and her smeared mascara only enhances her crazed appearance.

She's carrying my purse in one hand and something small that I can't quite make out in her other. Eyes livid, she charges toward me.

"Crap," I murmur when I realize exactly what she has in her hand.

"Vivian! Are you leaving?" She grimaces maniacally, heels clacking and hair flying out around her.

Easton takes my arm, moving toward the exit ahead of Cooper and Abby.

"Wait, Easton, this is about you too—at least I assume these are for you, but with girls like her, you just never know." She speaks loudly, carrying her voice to as many people as possible, and moving swiftly across the crowded room. People part before her like she's royalty, or it might just be the shock at seeing her looking like this. Heads at nearby tables turn and a few dancers stop and look our way. She grabs Easton's wrist, turns his hand palm up, and slaps the small box of condoms into it. My face feels hot when I cover it with my hand, and I bet my cheeks are cherry-red.

Trista's preening like a rooster, her big chest puffed out, her arms akimbo. "Her purse was in the bathroom, and because I'm such a kind-hearted girl, I didn't want her to forget it." She bats her eyes and tilts her head, sporting a little smile that adds to her crazed expression. "There are three in there." She points to the tiny box with the corners crushed from her grip. "Apparently, she has big plans for you tonight! Vivian, I knew you were a freak, but I had no idea you're a slut, too!" Throwing back her head, she laughs then looks around to include as many people in her 'kind' gesture as possible. Some whisper and point; you'd think by now it wouldn't bother me.

Just like then, I feel my anger and power building. This girl is really dense. I would assume after just having her ass zapped in a bathroom stall she'd be leery of me, at the very least a bit cautious and unsure. Hello! I think her hair's even still smoking slightly. I grit my teeth till my jaw aches.

"Well, that's certainly something you'd know about, Trista," Abby says, stepping again into Trista's face and snatching my purse from her hand. I'd laugh if I weren't so humiliated.

Easton closes his hand over the box and puts his arm around my shoulders. Rolling his eyes, we head toward the door. Good ole Easton. Does anything ruffle this guy? He's seen me hanging like an ornament on a tree, been the boy in the bubble above my bed, and now I've embarrassed him in front of the entire junior and senior classes at *the* most important social event of a teenager's high school career. He may be more perfect than I had thought. I'd bend him over my arm in one of those old Hollywood kisses if this weren't totally the wrong moment.

But Trista's not finished with either of us. She stomps behind us like an agitated pit bull refusing to let go, taunting me, looking very different from her grand entrance earlier tonight. Her dress is wrinkled and dirty with a spot of something wet near the bottom hem. She's taken off her shoes, maybe to keep up with us, and her makeup is smeared garishly.

"Vivian, we're more alike than you think." Ignoring her is not an option. Her voice grows louder and louder, and she's practically jogging to keep up with us.

When we open the gym doors, a jacketless Dillenger is closing the door of Trista's car. He is weaving toward us, refilling his flask from a near-empty bottle of clear liquid, vodka I presume. Tossing the bottle into the grass near the door, he says, "What's goin' on, Trista? Why you with these losers?" Even though his tie's slightly crooked and his voice is slurred, he's steadier than I had at first thought. He grabs Abby by the upper arm.

"Where you think you're goin'? You're my ride tonight."

Cooper bristles and steps closer to Dillenger whose red face grows even darker.

"You can ride home with Trista or Darcy." Abby's voice is loud and clear, not at all like before. She pushes against him when he leans in toward her, and she makes a face at the alcohol smell of his breath.

"That's not what I'm talking about, and you know it. I've put up with you for weeks. Now I want my reward." He jerks Abby forward, and I don't know if her gasp is from pain or from outrage at his words.

Before I can move at all, Cooper swings and connects his fist with Dillenger's face. Blood spurts from Dillenger's nose as Coop grabs his collar, pulls Dillenger toward him, and punches him again. Dillenger's knees buckle, and he falls face forward on the asphalt. His nose will definitely never be the same again.

Cooper wipes his hand on his pants, straightens his hat, and gently pulls Abby into his side. "You okay?"

Abby's face glows, but she just nods vigorously. She grabs his hand and turns it over assessing his scraped knuckles. "Your hand! You're hurt." She presses it close to her chest and gazes adoringly into his eyes. His cheeks turn a deep crimson.

"It's okay, but, uh, maybe you should... handle me gently tonight." He grins. "You wanna go?" Abby nods again, beams radiantly, and starts pulling him toward her car. "We're leavin', Easton." But Cooper isn't looking at either of us, just Abby's retreating back.

"Call you later, V." She only has eyes for her hero as she walks away waving over her shoulder.

Trista, who's been watching all this from the sidelines, runs over to Dillenger where he's moaning on the ground. She helps him to a sitting position and gives me the death stare as she rises to face me.

Easton holds out his hand as if to keep her at a distance. "It's over, Trista. You've had your fun and caused enough damage for one night." We turn toward his SUV again.

Without warning, Trista slams into me from behind and propels me to the ground.

CHAPTER TWENTY-FOUR

THE FALL KNOCKS THE AIR from my body. I can't breathe because Trista's sitting on my back. From the corner of my eye, I see her fist coming toward my head. The impact scrapes my face against the asphalt. Then I realize my arms and hands are trapped at my sides by her knees. I still feel the power building in my chest. I wiggle my right hand in an attempt to free it. She's screaming, but my brain can't register what she's saying.

Easton's voice reaches me; he's yelling something and trying to pull her off of me. I manage to turn my head between blows and see a battered Dillenger rushing Easton, tackling him at the waist. When she tugs my head back again, I grab her lower leg with my luminous hand and send a jolt great enough to force her off of me. I push myself to my feet as she flops sideways and howls in pain.

My gorgeous silver-white gown is filthy, ripped and snagged where my knees hit the ground. I think of all those extra hours Aunt Charlotte had to work to buy me this dress and the proud look in her eyes as she helped me get dressed earlier. Most of my hair has fallen loose from the pins and tumbles down my back, and my head throbs from the punches while my left ear rings slightly. The scratches on my cheeks burn when I raise my hand and touch them.

Easton and Dillenger are rolling on the ground, throwing and dodging fists. Trista's on her butt holding her injured leg where I can see red welts like those on Betty's arm.

"What did you do?" She stands. I close my eyes, struggling for composure. "I was so right! First the bathroom and now this! You're a total freak, and by tomorrow, *everybody's* gonna know!"

The starburst explodes inside of me.

"Trista." My voice is astonishingly calm. When she turns back, I open my eyes. Not only is my vision tunneled precisely, but I also see the bull's-eye pulsing from her head and heart. Everything turns blue.

Trista's mouth hangs open; her breathing's heavy, her eyes enormous in a face gone white. "You're… you're…" She pivots and sprints toward the gym, moving remarkably fast. I shake my head and click my tongue like a frustrated babysitter.

"Trista, Trista, Trista, you can't leave now. The fun's just starting."

I whip my hand in her direction, and blue current shoots toward her, wrapping around her waist like an electric rope. Jerking my hand back, I pull her, heels dragging, to within three feet of me. By this time the boys have stopped fighting and stand watching, dazed expressions mirroring Trista's. She has yet to realize that struggling is useless because she's trying to pull away, running in place like some bizarre cartoon. I twirl my finger, and she jerks around facing me.

Her pulsing energy spots flash a fast-paced tempo with her increased fear. "Aw, are you scared of the freak, Trista? Maybe you're smarter than I gave you credit for because you should be." On the edge of my control, I whisper the last part about an inch from her petrified face. I don't feel like myself. I'm powerful and very, very pissed. I am the puppet master. I can make her do whatever I want, and there's not a damn thing she can do to stop me.

Easton suddenly appears at my side. "Vivian, you have to calm down and let her go. I know she doesn't deserve it, but you're a better person than she is." He caresses my back, rubbing lightly. I clutch my fist tightly and squeeze the band around her boa-constrictor style before turning to Easton.

"I don't want to be a 'better' person right now. I want to punish her for all those people like me that she's hurt over the years. Don't worry. I won't damage her too much, just a teensy bit." I pinch my fingers together, and Trista whimpers as she's jerked over at the waist, mimicking my finger movements.

Eyes grave, mouth stretched rigidly, he tenderly strokes my face. Crap! Why'd he have to do that? I groan on an exhaled breath. "Vivian, please stop, if not for her then do it for me." Hair mussed from the fight and eyes pleading, he turns my shoulders slightly toward him.

"Dammit! Alright! I'll clip the string for you, not her! But first, I've got to do one more thing." I fling her to the doorway of the gym, enter her mind, and release the energy field. I'm now controlling her through mental force, not as gratifying, but just as effective. This is going to be entertaining.

Her eyes become empty as I hurl open the doors and simultaneously pull the plug on the band's sound equipment. A chorus of confused voices erupts from the open doorway. I amplify her voice so that it may be heard distinctly across the stuffy gym. I want the whole world to hear this.

"I'm very sorry to all of the people I've hurt. I'm a fake and a liar, and so are all of my phony friends. You are all better than I am and should never be intimidated by me again. Ignore me like I don't exist. It's what I deserve." Her voice is clear though her expression is blank.

I slam the doors closed and yank her back to me. "I know you won't remember this after I turn your prom memory to mush, but" —I shrug and smirk— "I just can't help myself." I punch her in the face with the force of a 'normal' girl—okay, maybe a little more than that but not enough to do permanent injury.

I rub my hand and pull from her brain, giving her a moment of lucid thought so that she will at least know for this moment that I have done this to her. Then looking directly into her furious face, I wipe her memory.

Plucking the one remaining orchid from my hair, I tuck it behind her ear into her semi-fried hair. "Who's the freak now?"

I leave her blinking in confusion.

CHAPTER TWENTY-FIVE

AFTER I FUZZ DILLENGER'S memory into a drunken haze, Easton tugs me into a jog toward the SUV. "Now would probably be a good time to leave."

He opens my door, and I climb inside. As he's getting in behind the wheel, I pull down the lighted vanity mirror expecting to find an extra from *Night of the Living Dead* staring back at me, but when I examine my face, the scratches are gone. Only dried blood smears remain. I push aside my torn dress, and the raw abrasions that should cover my knees from Trista's football tackle have vanished as well. I'm still bent searching my legs as Easton speeds out of the parking lot. I'm not sure where we're headed, but we're going to get there fast.

"You alright?" His eyes flick from me to the dark road ahead. His tense voice draws my attention, and I sit up but can't bring myself to look at him. I'm mortified by everything that's happened since Trista showed the world my Aunt Charlotte's well-meaning but completely misplaced surprise.

"Vivian"—he pulls into the parking lot of a fast food restaurant—"answer me."

I sigh heavily. This evening was going to be so great. We would dance and laugh, make some memories. Well, that we at least did do, just not the kind I was hoping for. It wasn't supposed to end with me nearly killing a girl. I look back at the mirror and finish plucking the pins and clips from my destroyed hair. Running my hand through it, I try to shake loose some of the tangles.

When at last I can avoid it no longer, I twist toward him. Looks like I fared much better than him. His left eye shows signs of bruising and will probably be black tomorrow, and his upper lip has a tiny cut near the corner. Both hands are scraped across his knuckles and down a couple of his fingers, and small spots of blood stain his cuffs. I want to take him in my arms and squeeze away any pain. I skim my fingers soothingly over his lips and eye. He rubs his face against my palm, aqua eyes serious.

"You're hurt." I'm stating the obvious, but what can I say knowing I'm responsible for spoiling my modelesque boyfriend's face.

"It's nothing, babe. What about you?" He studies my hand for injuries then he lifts the hem of my dress to check my knees, making my body tingle when he touches first one then the other leg. As he moves his fingertips over my once scraped cheek, he whispers in awe, "Amazing. You really are like some superhero, Vivian."

My hair tumbles to hide my face when I drop my head. He pulls his hand away but rests it on my still bare knee. His words are sweet, but he doesn't understand the guilt I feel. I ruined all of our evenings, and I could have really injured Trista, who deserves it, but that's beside the point. "No, Easton, if it weren't for you I might've actually hurt Trista. I was naïve to think I could control my power and be responsible with it. I need to go away, Easton, be away from other people."

Taking a shuddering breath, I close my eyes knowing I'm right. I have to leave even if that means leaving Aunt Charlotte behind. After all, she didn't sign up for this. I was dumped on her without a choice. She deserves to have the life she chooses, not the one forced upon her, and Easton... he's completely free. He definitely doesn't deserve the responsibility of having a volatile girlfriend, and sooner or later, he'll figure that out.

He starts to speak, but I lift my head and meet his distressed expression. "Easton, I'm right. Aunt Charlotte, Abby, you—I hurt everyone who makes the mistake of getting too close to me. Just look in the mirror! It's literally written all over your face. And

Abby's constantly punished because she's brave enough to be my only friend. Aunt Charlotte, she picked up and moved, leaving the life she'd created, to save me from, what? Some unknown threat I only remember in my nightmares. I have to leave all of you before anyone gets truly hurt... or worse." Unable to stand his cool gaze, I turn my face and look out at the cars parked near us. My throat tightens.

"No, Vivian." His voice is soft but firm. I'm about to argue with him when I hear his door open and close. Suddenly, he's in front of me, holding open my door. He turns me to face him. "No, I refuse to accept that. You, you're like no one else." He grabs both of my hands.

"That's an understatement," I murmur.

"Stop, it's your turn to listen." Surprise causes me to sit up straight, jerk my head back, and peer into his face. "I will *never* leave you. Most adults say we're too young to be in love, but I don't care. You have an awesome power that could easily destroy anybody in your path, but I don't care. You want to leave, but I don't care. You're wrong, and I won't let you leave like this. We'll talk to Charlotte and Abby. But I can tell you they'll agree with me. After, if you still want to go, I'm going with you. I love you even if you aren't ready to say it back to me."

I should tell him there's no way he can come with me, and I'm shaking my head, but throughout his speech, he's moved nearer, pushing up my dress hem so that he's standing between my knees. He edges closer and tugs me fully against him with his hands against my lower back. I smell his cologne; I feel his rapid heartbeat. The material of his jacket is scratchy against my legs.

"Vivian," he breathes my name close to my mouth. Running my hands up his arms, I twine my fingers behind his neck and pull his face to mine. We're about to kiss, but an older couple, carrying cups of coffee, walks past us, reminding us where we are.

The old man, with his belted, high-waist pants and polyester striped shirt, shuffles by, eyes diverted from us, but his wife, a shriveled woman with severe features and too much red lipstick, can't help but 'tsk.'

"Young people today have no manners. Really! Acting like that in public!"

"Oh, Margie, leave 'em alone. Can't you remember those days? Maybe I should remind you." And he pats her on the butt.

"John," she gasps, then giggles like a girl.

We're both smiling as he opens the passenger door on a big RV. He helps her inside then waves back at us as he gets behind the steering wheel and drives away.

Easton clears his throat, but one corner of his mouth quirks up. "Guess we should save the kiss for later."

"Probably a good idea."

CHAPTER TWENTY-SIX

AFTER BEING MILDLY GROSSED out by the old couple and realizing neither of us had eaten since lunch, we went into the restaurant, and despite the strange looks we got from the manager, we had a nice meal even if it was only a burger and fries. We also used the opportunity to clean up a little in the restrooms, washing away the blood. I finger-combed my hair and ripped off the ruined part of my gown from the knees down since it was already so tattered. I winced a little as I tossed the frayed remnant in the restroom trash bin. It'd been so lovely, all shimmering and pristine. Damn Trista! She ruined everything.

But I got a tiny bit of revenge myself tonight. She may not remember being spun like a top or apologizing to an entire gym full of people, but come Monday morning, she'll know what it feels like to be the outcast, the freak, when everyone whispers behind their hands and turns to stare as she walks down the halls. She won't be able to hide behind her expensive clothes and good looks. Teenagers aren't real good at forgetting. They'll eventually lump her in with the other tragically pathetic and move on to the next big thing.

We're driving to my house, and I can't help but chuckle when I remember how surprised she looked. Easton, having opted for his white tank undershirt instead of his jacket and dress shirt, glances over at me.

He smiles. "What's so funny?"

"I'm just thinking about the day Trista's going to have on Monday." But then I remember the box, that tiny little square of embarrassment, and even though my cheeks burn with humiliation, I need to say something, to know what he's thinking about it, about me. I hope he doesn't assume I meant to *need* them.

"Uh, Easton, about the, uh, the box that Trista found in my purse." I stare out the front window, suddenly fascinated by the trees that I can't even make out in the dark. He doesn't say anything, but I see him grin from the corner of my eye. He's not going to make this easy.

"They weren't mine, well, not exactly." I'm gesturing crazily, trying to make my hands say what my mouth can't seem to get right. "What I mean is they were *mine*, but uh, you see Aunt Charlotte thought I might need them, so..."

His sputtering laugh stops me mid-explanation. "Your Aunt Charlotte gave them to you?"

"Well, yeah." I bristle a tiny bit and finally glance at him. "She was trying to be protective." At his increased laughter, I realize what I've just said. "Bad choice of words. What I meant was motherly. She was trying to be motherly."

"Ha! Not many 'mothers' are handing out condoms." Air quotes, he knows I hate that. That just riles me up more.

"Maybe not, but she didn't want you taking advantage of me, and..."

Again, he interrupts, a little agitated himself. "Take advantage of you? Vivian! Is that what she thinks of me? Is that what you think of me?"

"No! No! That's not what I meant. Crap, this isn't coming out right at all. Okay, let me start over." I take a deep breath. "She wanted me to be responsible if I decided, uh, that is if we decided to..." I raise my eyebrows and tilt my head. I refuse to say it aloud.

"To?" He's smiling once more, playing dumb, but I won't let him have the upper hand. He narrows his eyes and quirks his full lips.

"To make a bad decision." And smirk back at him.

But in that tight shirt pulling across his pecs and abs, his defined biceps bulging a tiny bit as he pulls into my driveway, that 'decision' doesn't seem like such a bad idea after all.

After he stops the SUV, puts it in park, and switches off the ignition, he doesn't speak or smile not even after he opens my door, and I get out. He looks pissed, great.

When he closes the door, I touch his bare shoulder. "Easton, I was only kidding. I'm sorry. Don't be angry with—"

He grabs me around the waist and jerks my chest to his then leans me back against the passenger door, the window cold on my rapidly heating skin. He scorches me with a sultry smile and kisses me hard, a thorough, needy kiss that makes me breathless and leaves no doubt what he's thinking.

While I blink up into those Caribbean-Sea eyes and struggle to collect my wits, he grins devilishly and says, "Bad decision, huh?" He moves to my neck where he nibbles and nips softly before he moves to my face again. "Judging by your reaction, I seriously doubt I'd be taking advantage of you."

I giggle. "Point taken. You may be right." Then I kiss him until my palm shines so brightly I'm afraid I'll accidentally burn him. When I fist my hand tightly between us, he pulls back.

"What? What's wrong?" He's panting slightly, and knowing I'm the cause of that, leaves me shaky.

Glancing down at the blue glimmer, I purse my lips. "I'm never gonna be able to control this with you around." I poke his chest lightly with my finger and pretend seriousness.

"We better practice a whole lot more then." His face is stern, but his eyes smile.

I push him slightly and grab his wrist to look at the time on his watch.

"Well, as much as I really, really want to, according to your watch, Romeo, it's past my curfew. Some of us have those you know. We better go inside before Aunt Charlotte sends out a search party or starts thinking I'm being taken advantage of." Hand-in-hand, we're both smiling walking to the porch. But as I get closer, I lose my humor.

The hidden key's no longer hidden. It's in the door lock, and the door is wide open. There's no light inside. Aunt Charlotte usually leaves a couple of lamps on at night. From the dark interior I vaguely see an overturned chair. Easton sees it, too, and pulls me back. But I yank my hand and run through the living room to the kitchen. I flip the light switch, but when it doesn't work, I open my still radiant palm and form a small glowing sphere as a makeshift flashlight.

The table's turned over, and one of our chairs is broken. A shattered mug lies in a puddle of coffee near the chair, Aunt Charlotte's chair. She must have been drinking coffee trying to stay awake to wait up for me.

"Aunt Charlotte!" I frantically scream her name and spin in a circle, running from room to room, the stillness my only response. Nothing. No Aunt Charlotte.

I scream into the silence.

CHAPTER TWENTY-SEVEN

"THEY'VE FOUND US." That's the only explanation. The men from my dreams, the men who were chasing my mother and me, have kidnapped Aunt Charlotte. Fear and uncertainty make my voice tense. I'm sitting in the remaining kitchen chair with my head in my hands.

When Easton returns, flashlight in hand from searching the rest of the house, he secures the back door and stands facing me in front of the sink, hands on the counter. I'm reminded of the day I had to explain to Aunt Charlotte about my fight with Betty Sanders. Just thinking of her alone with them brings tears to my eyes, but I refuse to let them fall. Instead, I set my face, my lips in a stern line, and grit my teeth. This is entirely my fault. I've brought monsters to our home, monsters seeking a monster, and Aunt Charlotte is the victim. I can't sit by and let this happen. Whoever these people are, they are definitely stronger than her and definitely dangerous. I try to remember details from my dream. They had radios and guns, outfitted like an army.

"Vivian! Vivian!" Easton's snapping his fingers in front of my face, and when I pinpoint him through tunneled, white vision, my palm is burning the table. Lifting it from the surface of the table, I notice that a smoking, black mark remains.

"Vivian, this is not your fault." He pulls me to my feet with his hands on my upper arms. "You didn't do this. Do you hear me?" I'm looking through him, plotting a rescue that doesn't involve Easton. No way I'm letting him go with me.

"I have to find her, Easton."

"We should call the police, leave this up to them." He's trying to be helpful, but he just doesn't get it.

"The police? Easton, these people hunted me and my mom down until she killed herself to save me! Aunt Charlotte changed our names to escape them!" I give him my back and run my hands through my hair. "And I've somehow led them right to us after eleven years of hiding!"

"You don't know it's the same people, and how could you have led them here?" The pleading tone of his voice breaks my heart because I know it must be tonight. I have to leave him behind.

Facing him again I lower my voice and draw a calming breath to make him think he's going to win this round until I come up with a plan. "Easton, you're probably right. I don't know how it happened, but it's terribly coincidental that they suddenly show up after I start really using my powers. Don't you think?"

"Yeah, maybe, I don't know, Viv, but you can't go off unprepared and pissed thinking you can take on these people. We don't even know where they've taken her." He sits in the chair I've vacated and seats me on his lap. He holds me as though he knows it's for the last time. "What do we do now? Wait?" He doesn't sound scared, just determined.

"*We* don't do anything. I wait; *you* leave. Go home and stay there. I couldn't live with myself if you got hurt or went missing, too." It kills me to say the words, and I'm almost hoping he doesn't listen to me, forces me to take him with me, because I am scared, scared I will be unable to save Aunt Charlotte. He gives me mental strength and saying goodbye will be excruciating.

"Not gonna happen, so get that thought outta your head." Sliding off his lap, I start for the stairs leading to my room.

"We should change clothes. There's no predicting what the next few hours will bring. Do you have other clothes?" I have to get away from him for a minute to come up with a plan.

"Yeah, I've got my practice gear and shoes in the back of my vehicle." He rises to get them but stops and lays his hand on my shoulder. "Promise me you'll still be here when I come back inside, that you aren't planning on ditching me and going alone." He already knows me too well.

I can't look at him when I say, "I'll be here, Easton." He lifts my hair and kisses the back of my neck. My traitorous body reacts with a tremor all the while my mind's shrieking Aunt Charlotte's name. I try to convince myself that I'm not lying, and technically, I'm not. I will be here when he returns, but he's definitely not going with me. I just don't know yet how I'll ditch him. He'll never agree to let me do this without him, and there's not going to be anything remotely safe about what I'll have to do. These men wanted to abuse my mom's power, or they wanted to eliminate it. Either way, I won't be getting out of this thing unscathed. I just hope I can get Aunt Charlotte first.

After I get upstairs, I start toward the bathroom for a fast shower. I have no idea how I'll even find Aunt Charlotte. Will they call? Send a message? Have some guy bring one of her fingers in a box? OMG! I'm going to hyperventilate. What if I miss their communication while I'm in the shower? What if they attack Easton?

Forget the shower.

I wash as quickly as I can and dress in jeans and a t-shirt. I don't usually wear my shoes in the house, but I lace up my tennis shoes in case I need to leave in a hurry, and I pull my tangled auburn hair into a messy bun.

I spot my backpack and empty it, thinking to bring some supplies. But what should I take to a kidnapping? I throw in a small first-aid kit and a change of clothes that will fit either Aunt Charlotte or me, then I run downstairs. As I'm squeezing in some bottled water and granola bars, Easton walks out of the downstairs bathroom. He's changed into athletic pants, his practice shirt, and tennis shoes and is carrying the gear bag that he normally uses for after-school practice. I'm staring, trying to memorize his face, his body. He has something in his hand.

Setting his bag on the table, he holds out the thing which I now see is a photograph. "I had this in my bag. It's been in there awhile. I printed it from my phone but kept forgetting to give it to you. Figure I should just give it to you now." He shrugs and puts his hands awkwardly in his pockets, rocking slightly on his heels.

It's the lake picture, my big catch that day when Coop, Easton, and I went fishing; the photo Coop snapped with Easton's phone. "I thought about framing it as part of your birthday present. But that's two weeks away, and tonight seems like a good time." He shrugs again.

I stare at the photo, at our smiling faces, before Easton knew all my weirdo secrets, before Aunt Charlotte paid the price for loving me. A tear spills down over the contours of my cheek and across my lips. Its salty taste makes me feel even sadder somehow.

Easton reaches for my hands which shake so that the photo shakes, too. "What? What is it? I didn't mean to upset you." He stoops down to look into my still-lowered face.

I refuse to let his last memory of me be one of blotchy cheeks, a running nose, and watery eyes, so I swipe at the tears with the hand that I pull from his hold and give him a smile.

"Gee, I hadn't realized how bad my hair looked that day," I say, trying to make light of my emotions. I can't let him suspect why I am so upset by his thoughtful gift. He gives me a 'be serious' look.

"Just joking. It's probably the sweetest thing anyone's ever done for me. Thank you, Easton." I hug him, holding on for a minute longer than I should. To be accepted, to be loved, that's all I've ever wanted. I've finally found that, and now I have to give it up. Life's so unfair. I didn't ask to have a gift—a curse, a terrible curse that only hurts people whether I want it to or not.

He drags me close and kisses the top of my head. "I made a print for myself, so I made one for you, too. I thought you might want one since it's our first picture." His aqua eyes remind me of rainforest flowers.

"Yeah, it's great, really," I whisper, inhaling his scent.

"First of many, right?" He smiles softly, but all I can do is nod my head unenthusiastically, step from his arms, and turn for the living room.

Taking down the photo of Aunt Charlotte and my mom, I return to the kitchen and stow both in a small, zipper pocket on my backpack. When he peers at me questioningly, I create an excuse.

"It makes me feel closer to her." In reality, I want both photos with me when I make my exit and leave behind all the people I love. Even though he nods, his expression is uncertain, but when he opens his mouth to speak, the ringing of my cell phone causes us both to jump.

As I dig for the phone in my backpack, the sound jars the still house like a fire alarm in the middle of a deep sleep. I fumble the phone and nearly drop it after I finally slide my finger over the touch screen to answer it. Before I can say hello, a deep male voice answers slowly, a cultured, velvet timbre I did not expect.

"Vivian, inside your Aunt Charlotte's car is a preprogrammed GPS unit. It will bring you to us, to her. We will expect you soon."

"Who are you? Is Aunt Charlotte okay? Let me talk to her!" My voice sounds strained as I feel my body tingle to life.

"Soon, Vivian," the disembodied voice says with finality.

"No, wait!" But the only response is a beep as the line falls silent. Easton grabs the phone from my hand, looks at the front, and tries to get the call-back number from my call log, but these guys are way too smart for that, masking the call as a private number.

"I have to go, Easton." We stare into each other's eyes.

"Okay, where?" He grabs my backpack and turns for the door. I have to think fast to get away from him.

"No! I need something from my room." I hesitate because I haven't thought this far ahead. "Uh, they say there's a map hidden in the closet in my room. If you'll get it, I'll go start Aunt Charlotte's car, and you can meet me outside."

He wrinkles his brows and shakes his head. "Why are we taking her car?"

"I don't know, Easton. That's what they said to do. They… they've, uh, disabled it. I'm, uh, supposed to use my power to start it—to prove who I am I guess." I shake my head in frustration and grab my pack from him. "I don't know. We just have to hurry. Please, Easton, just get the map, okay?"

"Yeah, yeah, okay. Don't worry. I'll be right back." He speeds up the stairs. When he's almost to my bedroom door, I follow. Throwing shoes and clothes out of the way, he's searching the floor of my closet on his hands and knees as I reach the doorway.

Head jerking up in surprise, he says, "I thought you—" but I don't let him finish. Instead, I slam the door closed and create a force field in front of it to hold it shut. He crosses the floor swiftly and pounds on the door.

"Vivian! What are you doing?" He sounds angry, unlike I've ever heard him, even with Trista or Dillenger. Realization dawns. "You tricked me? What's going on? Let me out!"

"Easton, it's the only way. You can't come with me. I won't take that chance." I place my hand on the door knob. I have no idea if this will work, but I have to secure the door so that it will stay closed when I'm gone. I send heat pulsing through my hand until the knob is sizzling orange and yellow. The mechanism is destroyed, and the knob is melting to the metal plate where it meets the door. It must be glowing on his side as well.

"Vivian! Stop! Don't think you'll get rid of me this easily! Vivian, please!" And his voice is so high-pitched and pleading that I almost cave and turn him loose. When I'm sure the metal's completely ruined, I withdraw my hand from the knob.

"I'm so sorry, Easton. I just want one person I love to be safe." I put my forehead and hand against the door.

"Vivian, please don't..." His voice catches, and he draws in a shuddering breath. "Don't do this alone. I *need* to go with you. I *need* you. I can't stay here knowing you're there. Please."

A tear drops off my nose. "Easton, I'm letting you go."

He rattles the door, banging and pounding again with his fists and shoulder. He curses and kicks, and even though the ancient door creaks, it holds firm. When he speaks again, his voice sounds as though he is now sitting on the floor. I picture him there, his knees on the scuffed wood, his hands flat on the door, his breath labored—beautiful and tragic.

"I will get out and find you. I can't let you go alone!"

My throat is so tight, I can barely speak. "You... you can't stop me."

I run downstairs and speed through the house to the sounds of Easton's struggles and irate yelling. I race outside and go to his SUV. Eventually, he will get out even if he has to use his cell to call Cooper, but I don't want him following me anytime soon. I look up at the sound of my window being raised.

Head hanging out, he yells down, "Dammit, Vivian! Just listen to me! The two of us will work better together, stand a better chance of rescuing Charlotte. Stop for a second and listen!"

The cloudy sky covers the moon and makes his features unclear, but his voice echoes all his hopelessness because he knows I am leaving him behind.

Placing my hand on the hood of his SUV, I guiltily send a jolt powerful enough (hopefully) to disable the computer system in his vehicle and keep it from starting. I don't want to ruin his ride, but it's a small price to pay to keep him safe and sound.

"Vivian!" I go to Aunt Charlotte's car, open the door, and chunk my backpack in the passenger seat. Pausing for one last glimpse, I see the clouds part, and moonlight illuminates Easton's face where he still stands at the window, his breathing heavy.

"Vivian"—his voice is so ragged and pained I can barely make it out—"I love you."

I realize this is the moment I've waited all night to find—my last chance—and I open his mind to my own and say the words I should have been saying all along, the words my heart knew to be true from the first time we kissed.

I love you too, Easton.

CHAPTER TWENTY-EIGHT

"**TURN LEFT IN THIRTY FEET.**" The mechanical voice of the GPS grates on my already raw nerves. This little machine has been directing me for almost two hours. I have no idea where I'm going, and I'm too afraid to mess with the thing to find out. I'm pretty sure that I could press a couple of buttons, and it would show me the address of my destination, but if I somehow manage to screw it up, Aunt Charlotte will pay the price for my failure to show.

I'm not even sure this car's going to make it. These people didn't plan very well, or they just didn't pay attention to the condition of Aunt Charlotte's car. Had they looked at the interior they could see it's on its last leg. The driver's seat is ripped from years of sliding in and out of the car. The dash is cracked and faded from too many hours parked in the sun. The radio's broken, not that I'd be able to concentrate on music right now anyway, and the headliner sags near the back glass.

At least it's clean, though. Aunt Charlotte's a bit obsessed with cleanliness. No soda bottles or napkins litter the ragged black carpet, and very little dirt covers the console. Some photo booth pictures stuck in the dash behind the steering wheel are the only paper in the car. The pictures are of Abby and me, making goofy faces. Aunt Charlotte had taken us out of town to shop over Thanksgiving break a couple of years ago, but when we'd tried to shop on Thanksgiving day none of the stores at the outside mall were open yet, so we'd climbed in the booth and snapped the photos to have something to do. We were freezing and had all bought new fuzzy hats when we'd arrived in town the day before. Those stupid hats made us look slightly crazy and very 'touristy'. At the bottom of the set, the last picture, all three of us had squeezed into the tiny space, and Aunt Charlotte had put her arms around our necks, accidentally bumping our heads together. We were all laughing hysterically when the camera clicked. I'd forgotten about these pictures until just now. It was the best Thanksgiving break I ever had.

The tears try to come, but I can't let them. If I start, I'll be too emotional when I finally get to Aunt Charlotte, and I need to be ready for whatever I'm going to find. I have to free her then convince her to let me leave. Leaving her will be so much harder than leaving Easton, but I have no choice. If I have to lock her up like I did Easton, then so be it. This kidnapping just proves that I can't stay, not if I want to keep her safe.

Aunt Charlotte's been the only mom I've really ever known. Even though I have a few memories of my actual mother, I can't say they're pleasant. Sleeping in a car, checking into seedy motels, eating ravioli from a can, not exactly Mother's Day card material. When I remember birthday parties, it's Aunt Charlotte I see. When I remember scraping my knees, it's Aunt Charlotte who bandaged them. When I remember bedtime stories, it's Aunt Charlotte who read them. She's... my mom. I *have* to get her out. Then I have to leave her behind.

*   *   *

After another hour or so, the robotic voice announces, "Destination ahead." By now, it's nearer to morning than to night, and I should be feeling the effects of sleeplessness, but I'm too wired for that. With every mile, every minute, my anxiety and adrenaline have increased. About ten minutes ago, I turned into a park entrance. From the looks of the place and the barely-hanging gate I'd say it's been shut down for a while. It's the kind of place teenagers break into, so they can party and have sex. The doors stand open on all the buildings, and every jagged, broken window's been used as target practice for rocks. The wind's kicked up, rattling the new leaves and scattering occasional small sticks, empty cans, and junk food wrappers.

From the darkness of the close trees, a man dressed entirely in black with at least two knives strapped to his legs and holding some kind of gun across his chest steps into the path of the car. Had I not been driving so slowly trying to focus on the area I would have hit him, and I jump when I see him. The headlights illuminate a badly scarred face, the bottom half appearing to have been burned at some time in the past.

He motions me down a side road, barely more than a trail, where trees twine together overhead and block most of the moonlight. The path opens into a clearing, and a dark, sluggish river cuts through it. It would make a perfect campsite with a tent and… and… this is it. This is the setting of my dreams where my mother died.

As I stop the car and get out, I scan the trees, and sure enough, several men crouch in the shadows. Based on their silhouette, they all appear to be carrying multiple weapons like the man at the end of the path.

No one approaches me, and I stand uncertain, slipping on the jacket Aunt Charlotte always keeps in the backseat. The wind yanks at my hair and plucks some of it from the holder. The tiny strands tickle my cheeks and nose, which only increases the eerie feeling I have. It's like I'm being drawn toward something indefinable, a moth to a flame, and we all know how well that always ends.

"Vivian"—the same smooth voice from the phone is coming from a group of trees directly in front of me—"how nice to see you again after all these years." His syrupy tone sends shivers down my back, and when he steps from the trees, I understand his meaning. I've seen him before. I'm staring into the black eyes from my nightmare.

He's tall, like a pro-ball player tall, with light brown hair. A small scar runs through his left eyebrow, splitting it into two-halves rather than a solid line. Other than the scar, his face is unwrinkled, and his features might be considered handsome if not for those soulless eyes, and the fact that he's obviously insane.

"I apologize for the setting, my dear. In our"—he clears his throat and smiles creepily—"line of work. We keep a low profile when-ever possible. Plus, a part of me enjoys the irony of it." He gestures, palms open and up, with both hands to indicate our surroundings. "You do recognize this place. Do you not?"

When I only glare as he inclines his head toward me, he continues, "I'll take that as a yes. In this very spot, I saw your lovely mother take her life, and I'd thought she'd taken yours as well. I, of course, quite happily discovered I was wrong when you gave me this." He runs his finger across the scar on his eyebrow and smiles again.

"You know, Vivian, you alone hold the honor of being the only person to ever mark me with a lasting reminder of a battle. Exploding that tree was truly remarkable and showed me the extent of your abilities. Perhaps it was because your precious mother had already injured me so severely, or"—he pauses thoughtfully—"perhaps, it's the unique connection you and I share." His words cause a shiver along my entire body this time. What connection? How could I possibly be connected to this, this, whatever he is? But I can't deny it though I want to badly. Since I stepped from the car, I've felt it, a weird pulling sensation, almost magnetic, toward something. Now I realize it's not something but someone.

"Either way, my dear, you did what no one else has managed to do in my rather extensive career. Congratulations." He bows his head slightly in acknowledgment of my success I suppose.

Finding my voice, I ask, "Where's Aunt Charlotte?"

"Patience, my dear, all in good time." He wags his finger at me.

"I'm not your 'dear.' Stop calling me that. Where is she?" My anger is beginning to overcome my fear, and my palm begins to glow. In the predawn darkness, the blue light radiates.

"Oh, but you are, Vivian. You just don't know it yet." He turns his head toward my palm. "Extraordinary. It is quite extraordinary how easily and quickly you can manifest your power. Your mother took a bit longer, had to really push her to get her going. But then again, you are special even among your own family."

I so want to know what he's talking about, but getting Aunt Charlotte is more important at the moment. He's trying to rile me with all this talk of my mother, and honestly, it's starting to work. I can't give him any more of an advantage by losing my temper. At the moment, the deck is stacked in his favor, and I can't win. Then again, a good bluff never hurt. Gotta make him think I'm more confident than I am.

"I don't give a damn about your opinion of my power. Just give me Aunt Charlotte, and no one will get hurt. We'll get back in this car, drive away, and forget all this."

He laughs, loudly. So much for my bluff.

"You are most assuredly not in a position to make threats. As powerful as you may be, you will never make it out of here alive unless I allow it. And who says I haven't already done away with the little problem of your Aunt Charlotte?"

I clench my jaw and step toward him. Although he stands his ground, he flinches almost imperceptibly. Maybe *he's* the one trying to bluff *me*. I open my mind and attempt to penetrate his, but he shakes his head and wags his finger again.

"Uh, uh, uh, none of that, my dear. You'll have to do better than that I'm afraid, though I must say your influence is very strong. But"—his lips become a line, and his brow wrinkles—"you'll find mine is much stronger."

With that a force like a sledgehammer slams into my mind. Images of dying men, burning houses, and frightened faces flash into my head. It's so intense I actually stagger backward and land against the car fender. These aren't just random pictures he's created. These are memories, his memories of the things he's done. When I regain my balance, I push him out of my mind and try to block his access to my thoughts, easier said than done.

"You are unquestionably strong. I can feel you pushing me out, and I will let you win, for the moment." He steps within two feet of me. With his black clothing identical to that of his men and his black eyes, he could easily blend with the night. He reaches out to touch my cheek, and I jerk away. He looks... hurt?

From the angle of his head and the sweep of his eyes I'm guessing he's studying my face, but it's impossible to know for sure since his eyes aren't human. Is he studying me? It makes me squirm nervously.

"I want to see Aunt Charlotte. Let me see her."

"But I am enjoying this little reunion of ours immensely." He sighs. "Oh, very well." Turning to two men standing to his left, he commands, "Bring her out."

He looks back at me. "You will be civil of course. If you choose not to do as you are told, you won't like the results I'm afraid." The men move toward a van some distance away and open the doors.

"Vivian!" I whip my head in the direction of Aunt Charlotte's voice. She's wearing her favorite pink satin pajamas that I bought her for her birthday last year. She is barefoot, and her long, red braid swings down her back. The two men holding her arms are battle-scarred like the others I've seen. One has a diagonal slash from his temple to his cheek. The other wears a pirate patch and holds his right arm at a strange angle as though it has been broken and poorly set. Their grips tighten when she calls my name and struggles against them.

I start toward her, but Black Eyes stops me without touching me, another show of his power. Resisting physically does absolutely no good, but I do it anyway, jerking my shoulders and arms to no effect. When I stop moving, he releases me and laughs.

"Are you finished?" he jeers.

"I haven't even started." Without looking at him, I jerk my hand forward in the direction of the men holding Aunt Charlotte. A blinding flash of white shoots out and hits one man square in the chest. The force propels him backward at least ten feet. Moving quickly I aim for the second one, but he dives to the side, taking a screaming Aunt Charlotte with him.

I pivot toward Black Eyes, intending to do the same, when I am suddenly propelled back into the car again by an invisible slam to the chest. Before I can catch my breath, I'm launched into the air by a wind as powerful as a cyclone and thrown back near the opposite tree line.

My legs and arms flail helplessly midair, and I land facedown so forcefully that my breath is knocked from me. It's impossible to resist the armed men who apprehend me and haul me to my feet. Sucking in huge gulps of air, I hang temporarily between them while my body tries to recoup. Before I can feel the oxygen rushing into my extremities, Black Eyes approaches me, commanding his soldiers as though we were never interrupted, same deep voice, totally unruffled.

Who is this guy? He has power, too, since he just tossed me like a twig, but what is it exactly? I can't fight him if I don't know what to expect.

He's shaking his head as though I'm his disobedient pet. "Vivian, I warned you, but you didn't listen. Perhaps we should start over. I haven't even introduced myself, and we're already at odds with each other. How could I have been so rude? I am Hoyt Matthews." He holds out his hand. As if I would ever shake it! When I simply stare and try to catch my breath, he frowns but gestures at the unseen troops apparently stationed around the clearing.

"My esteemed colleagues and I work for a very secret organization, and it's my, excuse me, *our* job to procure uniquely talented individuals, like you. Your family is closely tied to this organization, though you don't really know that—yet. I am extending an invitation to you to join us." He motions away the men holding me up and puts his arm around my shoulders, shoving me into his side. My unsteady legs are just now beginning to hold my weight again. He sits me on a stump nearby and kneels in front of me, taking my upper arms in his hands.

"Vivian, there is so much I can tell you about yourself, your family. I knew your father. Don't look so surprised, my dear. He was, after all, one of our group." And I don't know if he means this organization or that my dad had abilities like us. He continues before I can ask, and this is not the kind of guy I should interrupt at least not until I get my strength back.

Sighing again, he continues, "Your mother—that was unfortunate. She simply didn't understand. Had she given me a chance, well, this meeting would not have been necessary." His stony eyes bore into me, and I feel him probing into my brain, but I'm just too weak to stop him. "I know you. I know what it feels like to be the outsider, to not belong anywhere. You have few friends, and those you have don't completely trust or know you. People make fun of you, and you fear for their safety if you lose control. There is no one who understands as completely as I do."

He's right. I hate to admit it, but everything he's saying is true. These are the exact reasons I have to leave. Do I belong with him? Would I finally fit in? I would never have to worry about appearing normal or just like all the other sheep in the world. I could finally be free to live as myself. This man knows more about me than my own friends. He touches my hand, and I don't pull away this time.

"You unintentionally hurt everyone you love. You will never feel normal with them, even Easton."

Wait, Easton? He knows about Easton? Damn, he's using my mind against me! I can't believe I almost fell for his crap! What a rookie mistake. How could I be so stupid! I shake my head and smirk, yanking my hand away from his.

"You're good, but you already know that. You used my own feelings against me, and you almost had me, you bastard!"

"I? I am a bastard?" He tries to look insulted but fails. He only appears smug, arrogant because he knows I'm really at his mercy.

Ignoring the question, I allow my sarcasm full reign. If I'm about to die, I might as well play a few games myself. "Well, at least we agree on that." I can finally feel my arms and legs again, and the tingle comes from my power this time.

"Vivian, I may have borrowed Easton's name from your memory, but everything I've said is true. I have felt the same things you have felt. I've been alone and misunderstood. No one can understand unless they have also experienced what we have. I was exactly like you until I found my place leading these men. There are others of us out there, and you can join us." When he pauses, I rise and place my hands on my hips. Looking into those eyes reminds me of a moonless night when every corner, every shadow holds a threat. I shiver but pretend indifference.

"Give it up, Hoyt. Every teenager from the beginning of time's felt alone and misunderstood. It's the most normal feeling in the world." Do I really believe that every teenager feels exactly like me? Hell no, but I refuse to let this guy know that. He chuckles. He knows I'm full of it.

"You do have spunk, my dear. You are so like your father. He, too, thought to stand up and be the lone hero. *He* didn't learn in time that he needed this organization, that he needed *me*. Will you?" He steps back and raises his arms above his head. "Perhaps, you need a little more persuading." When he drops them, it feels as though all the wind in the world hits me in the chest, and I fly over the stump and smack the tree behind me. The bark scrapes my back as I slide down the trunk and hit the ground. He walks slowly toward me.

"I'm sorry, my dear, but really you left me no choice. If I can't convince you logically that we are your only option then"—he shakes his hands at his sides as though he's loosening them up—"I'm afraid I'll have to beat some sense into you."

Bracing myself with my hands, I come up to my knees, head down, eyes closed. This time I don't try to calm myself. I let the starburst explode and feel the heat vibrate through my arms and legs. My right palm pulses. When I open my eyes and raise my head, I lock on this man's energy fields, now gone entirely blue and throbbing rapidly. He's not as confident as he wants me to believe. I refuse to let him throw me like a beanbag again. His eyes meet mine.

"Come on, asshole. Let's do this." And I rise to my feet.

CHAPTER TWENTY-NINE

HOYT'S FACE IS SUDDENLY SERIOUS, and adrenaline causes his energy levels to climb. From across the clearing I hear Aunt Charlotte screaming.

"Vivian, no! Don't try to fight him! You'll be killed!" Even though I can't see her clearly, I can tell she's struggling with her captors from the strained tone of her voice.

Under my breath I mutter, "Thanks for the vote of confidence, Aunt Charlotte."

"Listen to her. She knows what she's talking about. After all, she is part of the reason I found you after all these years." I'm confused, and my expression must show it.

"Oh, you didn't know? My dear, really, I thought you were exceptionally intelligent, yet you couldn't figure this out? Maybe I *should* kill you—cull you from the pack—if you're that dim-witted."

At this point my hand no longer resembles my hand at all. In fact, I can't even see my skin. It's like a brilliant azure light bulb hanging from my arm where my hand should be. 'Kill me? Cull me from the pack'? Bring it, buddy.

"Your aunt's researching adventure a few weeks ago clued me into your whereabouts. Who else but Charlotte would be searching for the park rangers who found you or your social service file? We have members everywhere, Vivian. A thirty second phone call is all it took to begin my search for you again. I tried to find you as soon as I learned that your mother hadn't annihilated you all those years ago, but Charlotte took you away from me." He sighs almost nostalgically then his face becomes excited.

"Then you had that delicious power surge. Combine that with Charlotte's curiosity... you might as well have drawn me a map." His sinister look chills me and gives me a moment of doubt in my own abilities. I was right when I told Easton I had brought this evil to us. I signaled him that night when I lost control at the lake and drew the lightning into me. He tracked me somehow. For eleven years I hid it from everyone, and we were safe. The minute I started using it my life's been a freak show. Aunt Charlotte was right to tell me not to use it all these years.

"It was only a matter of time, actually. I knew you would grow too powerful to suppress it, and you will NEVER be able to hide from me. We belong together, united, my dear. Our connection is too strong."

When he approaches me this time, I'm ready. Slinging out my right hand, I shoot a beam of energy into his chest. Contact! He flies through the air. Grunting, he lands about seven feet away and throws up his hands to retaliate, but I don't give him the chance.

"Oh no you don't!" I sling another jolt as several of his men run toward me, guns drawn. I can't let them take me. I need leverage. Whipping out the same blue energy rope I used on Trista, I bind his arms and yank him toward me. When he's within arm's reach, I throw up my hand and manifest an energy shield, the same power bubble Abby and Easton have seen. From the safety of the shield, I see the soldiers raise their weapons and fire some kind of darts at us. But they all just bounce harmlessly away. I think I'm winning! I raise my arms up and propel us skyward. Hoyt's eyes are wide, shocked, his breathing fast.

"What have you done? How are you doing this?" His gaze flits frantically down at the rope and then around at the shield.

"Maybe you underestimated me. You should have done your homework." I grip him harder with the rope, causing him to grunt. He's panting shallowly with the force of the hold, but he's far from defeated. His black eyes lock on mine. Try as I might, I can't look away or even blink. His gaze is hypnotic like a cobra readying to strike.

You will release me.

He's in my head again, forceful and confident. I push hard, but I can't drive him out.

Vivian, let me go.

I can't speak; I can't move. I feel my resistance fading, myself fading.

Loosen the binding. That's it.

What? I loosened it? No! I try to tighten it again. Nothing, I can't even manifest it again.

Take me to the ground.

The ground... yes. Why am I in the air anyway? I can't remember.

Yes, my dear, that's it. We're almost back down.

I need to make my feet touch the ground.

Open the shield, Vivian.

The... the... shield...

"Vivian! Don't let them hit you with the tranquilizer darts!"

Who's screaming? I know that voice.

I look toward the sound and see a long, red braid. Her back is to me, and they are forcefully dragging her away, trying to shove her into a van. But that voice, that hair, are all the reminder I need to pull me back to myself.

"Aunt Charlotte!" I thrust Hoyt from my mind. The shield! I lift my hands to manifest it again, but he's too quick this time. He throws both hands forward, and I become a human discus again. Midair my brain jumps to action. I manifest the shield. Instead of being flattened on the ground, I land softly, protected by the energy ball.

"Take her from here!" Hoyt's totally lost it. He's screaming at his men, and the van spins its tires in the moist ground, trying to make a fast exit.

"No!" I can't let them take her again. Pointing both hands at a huge oak tree near the van, I send a massive wave. Blue sparks fly in every direction when the force hits the tree. A deafening crack then the tree falls, blocking the path of the van.

Brakes screech. The van reverses direction, so I do it again and block it from the back. This enormous chess game ends when Hoyt screams, "Enough!" He throws his arms skyward. The clouds swirl; the wind whips the tops of tall trees.

"Vivian, I wanted you to join us. A successful army needs leaders, and there are so few of us with special talents. These men are merely the castoffs, unwanted by others. They have no real gifts like you and me. I wanted this so badly, but you don't always get what you want." His eyes narrow. By now the wind is savage; even the soldiers have abandoned their leader, sheltering in the other vehicles scattered around. It tugs at my energy shield. "It's time for you to learn that lesson as well."

He flings his arms toward the van holding Aunt Charlotte. Like flipping a pancake, the wind tosses the van end-over-end, high into the air. Over the sound of the wind's fury, I hear Aunt Charlotte's scream mixed with that of his soldiers' inside.

I try to project the orb around the van to stop it before it hits the ground, but I'm not strong enough. I've depleted my energy supply. I stand helplessly by while the van crashes, glass shattering, near the river. It's on its side, and the smoking engine hisses as liquid leaks from somewhere in the van.

I break from my shield, pulling it inside, and race to the van. Peering inside, I see the two men hanging at odd angles, blood covering their upper bodies and pieces of glass embedded in their chests, arms, and faces. The latch on the van's back door is broken, and I climb inside the dark interior where I project a small energy orb for light.

When I see her, I collapse to my knees. She's lying on her side facing away from me, but blood covers the once pink pajama top as crimson pools beneath her. I crawl on hands and knees toward her. "Aunt Charlotte?"

Gently, I roll her into my arms. A large shard of glass glistens sickly from the center of her chest. There's a gash in her cheek, and her arms are a mass of nicks and cuts. When I say her name, her eyes flutter then open. She reaches up and touches my face, trying to comfort me with a smile. But the blood trickling from her lips makes me more afraid.

"Vivian, you're alive, thank God." Her eyes are drifting closed again.

"Aunt Charlotte! Open your eyes. Look at me! I'll fix this." But my heart knows it's a lie, and a tear slides down my cheek onto the hand she still has pressed weakly against my face.

"No, Vivian, not this time. Don't cry." She drags in a guttural breath, and the blood flows more freely from her mouth. Her hand falls as does her eyelids.

"Aunt Charlotte!" My voice chokes, and tears blur my vision. The effort it takes for her to drag her eyes open is painful to watch. She smiles sadly again.

"Go with them, Vivian. I can't leave you knowing you aren't safe, and they will never stop chasing you. Please" — she forces in another breath and coughs as blood spurts in tiny droplets — "promise me you won't fight them."

"I... I..." I can't do it. I can't promise her that.

With a quick, hard intake of air, her eyes widen, and she grabs my hand.

"No, don't leave me!" Then her lids close, and her head falls to the side as life leaves her body. It all happens so quickly. This wonderful woman is gone.

"I love you, Aunt Charlotte. I'm so sorry." I rock her lightly back and forth, back and forth, until I've lost track of how long I've been in the van. I think of all those hopes and dreams we had for our lives together, all the plans that will never come true. We were going to move when I finished high school, get an apartment in a city where I could go to college. I was going to get a part-time job to help with our bills. Our lives were going to be so perfect finally. Maybe deep down I knew those plans wouldn't ever happen because I'm not surprised, just terribly, terribly sorry.

I must not cry. I can't think of all we've lost. I can't let myself feel the misery that I know will come later. I can't think about it, any of it, the loss, the regret, the total failure. I must not break. I cannot — for her.

I lay her gently on her back, pull off the jacket, her jacket, and drape it over her face. I couldn't do it. I couldn't promise her that I wouldn't go after them. My last act with Aunt Charlotte, and I will have to disappoint her because I'm most definitely going to disobey her this time.

My body already shakes with the building force, and with it my tears vanish. There will be time to mourn later. Right now, I have work to do.

CHAPTER THIRTY

AS I EMERGE FROM THE VAN, I don't have to search to find Hoyt. He's standing just outside, surrounded by armed men. His face shows no remorse. I lock onto those evil eyes.

"You forced me into that, Vivian. In fact, your very existence has caused numerous deaths. First, the rangers who were unlucky enough to find you, next the social worker in charge of your file, even your beautiful mother's demise can be linked to you."

I flinch, looking down at Aunt Charlotte's blood still coating my hands and clothes, but everything he says is the truth. Still, that's not going to stop me from ripping his head off, slowly.

"Now, poor, tragic Charlotte who only tried to give you a normal life. A shame, a waste that didn't have to happen. You see why you belong with us? We"—he motions around with both hands—"will be your family." Smiling, he steps toward me, believing he's won. "I will teach you to harness your power. You have no idea what you can do." He chuckles. "You have no idea what other skills you possess. But I will teach you. You'll be my protégé."

His energy pulses fast. When I lift my eyes, I can no longer see in the typical sense. Just like the night of my power surge, the world is blue. Only energy fields exist, making my targets clear and distinct. "You may be right about everything. All those deaths, my mom, Aunt Charlotte." My voice catches slightly. I nearly choke on her name.

He smiles widely, so certain I'm giving in. When he reaches out his hands, I hold up my hand which radiates like an azure lantern despite, or maybe because of, Aunt Charlotte's blood.

"And I'm sure you can teach me a thing or two, but I have learned one thing about my abilities on my own. Sometimes I need a little recharge, and it doesn't necessarily take a stormy sky to draw lightning. Let me show you." With that, I throw my hand skyward. Jagged lightning cracks from the few clouds overhead and explodes a large tree behind the soldiers who scramble like ants in every direction, abandoning their leader. Shock flashes on Hoyt's face as he too jumps back from me.

"Did you like that? How about another demonstration?" This time I summon the lightning into my hand and fling it like a flaming basketball toward one of their vehicles parked near the forest. It flies into the surrounding trees, taking down several.

"Tranquilize her, you idiots!" Hoyt screams as he runs toward his men who don't seem to be thinking about their weapons, just saving their asses.

Again and again I fire energy into the trees, the vehicles, the groups of men. I refuse to think that I'm probably killing them. They are all responsible for Aunt Charlotte's death as far as I'm concerned, and they must all pay the price.

The lightning is fueling me, recharging me. He cannot stop me. I don't know if I can even stop myself. Screams and explosions fill the clearing, and I remember my last visit here. With the memory of my mom, my anger climaxes. "You killed them! You killed my family, you bastard!"

Rapid fire, I shoot again and again until fires burn all around like hell on Earth. Energy pulses still flash occasionally, but the number has decreased by half. Through the smoke and confusion, I locate Hoyt's energy signal, like a beacon calling me in. He's hunkered behind a fallen tree—the coward!

"Hoyt?" I call out singsong style. "Come out, come out wherever you are." I walk around the front of the van where I smell gas and oil still leaking from the vehicle. "You wanted to play, and here I am. That's not very nice. Didn't your mother teach you anything?"

From his hiding place, he taunts me, "Yes, Vivian, she did. Didn't yours?"

Oh no, he didn't just say that. Inhaling sharply I feel something snap inside of me. I have to end this, for my mom, my Aunt Charlotte, and myself. "Sorry, Aunt Charlotte."

Stepping around the front of the van, I lift my hand and fill it with power until it burns more vividly than any of the others I've thrown. I hurl it into the van. The fuel turns it into a gigantic bomb, and it explodes toward Hoyt's hiding place.

*   *   *

The quiet of Aunt Charlotte's car causes my ears to ring. Just like before I have no idea where I'm going except this time I also have no purpose. I didn't stick around after I tossed the van on Hoyt. I got in the car (the only vehicle left standing after my rampage) and took off. I have no destination and no plan. All I know is I have to get away from here.

Grabbing my backpack from the passenger seat where I flung it earlier, I dig in the front pocket for the two photos I placed there earlier. I stick both in the dash next to the photos of Aunt Charlotte, Abby, and me. These are the people I love most, the people I've hurt and can never see again.

The tears come regardless of how hard I push them away; the dam's broken. Like a flooded river I can hold them back no longer. Rain begins to splatter the windshield, and between the tears and Aunt Charlotte's worn out wipers, I'm forced to pull over at a fast food restaurant.

Where am I going? I can't go home. There's no home without Aunt Charlotte anyway. I won't go to Easton or Abby. Their safety must come before anything else. As I watch a little girl and her dad dash through the rain and into the restaurant, I know what I have to do.

If Hoyt knew my father, someone else must remember him, too. My mother met him while she was working as a waitress somewhere out West. She was a student at a small college. There have to be records. If I can discover where she went to school I can find where she worked, and maybe someone will remember her with my father. It's a long shot, but sometimes that's all you've got.

Hoyt hinted that my father was dead, but that could've been a lie. The word of a psycho isn't exactly reliable after all. If he is dead he could still have family. I might have a grandmother out there somewhere, and even if I can't stay with her or get too close to her, I can at least see her, possibly talk to her for a few minutes.

I have to try. I have to know — if for no other reason than to fill in the gaps of who I really am. I've thought about him a few times over the years, and tonight's just a reminder of all I've lost. If I can find some tiny trace of him, *anything*, maybe I can start rebuilding who I am. I can't move forward if I have no past.

A week ago I thought life was pretty bad. I didn't know if my best friend was a traitor, if she hated me, if she'd ever want to be my friend again.

A few hours ago I finally got revenge on the bitch that terrorized me for so long, and I was looking forward to seeing the reactions at school on Monday.

I had a boyfriend who was a fantasy, my white knight on a mission to rescue me and take me to his castle in the stars.

An hour ago I had an aunt who put me above everyone, everything else.

Now, I am alone.

EPILOGUE

SIRENS BLARE IN THE DISTANCE. The whirl of helicopter blades is much closer. Early dawn pinks the sky where black smoke billows from fires across the once peaceful clearing. With all the vehicles destroyed, the soldiers had had to phone for backup transport. The few men left alive efficiently gather the dead and the debris as much as possible. The scene looks like a war zone instead of a closed state park.

Between a blazing van and a charred fallen tree, a man stirs slowly. He's lying on his stomach, his back as burnt as the tree beside him. Holes in his clothing smoke, and when he tries to rise to his hands and knees, he falters and flops back to the ground.

A soldier limps over, holding his left leg where blood oozes over his fingers from a wound in his thigh. "Sir, sir, can you hear me?" He tries to kneel but grimaces from the pain in his leg and only manages to bend at the waist. When the soldier touches the man's shoulder, the man grabs the soldier's injured thigh in a surprisingly vicious grip considering the injuries to the man's back and arms. The soldier's face contorts in agony, and he can't stop himself from falling to the ground in anguish. "Stop, please, stop, sir! It's me. It's Hanson!" He grabs for the wound that now hemorrhages profusely.

The man loosens his hold but otherwise doesn't acknowledge the soldier.

Gasping violently from the pain and blood loss, the soldier addresses his leader again. "Sir, they're coming for us. The helicopters are nearly here, but so are the local authorities. We have to be gone before area law enforcement arrives." When he pauses, the sirens sound much louder.

"The girl?" The man's voice, typically deep and level, betrays his own suffering.

Like an omega wolf, the soldier lowers his head to his alpha, his tone begging and conciliatory. "No, sir, I'm sorry. She escaped." Looking around at the devastation, he continues nervously, "Maybe we should let this one go."

The man's head jerks up sharply. His eyes fly open. He focuses his obsidian gaze on the soldier.

"I *will* find her. She's my blood."

ACKNOWLEDGMENTS

Thank you, Olivia and Wyatt, my too often ignored children, and my hubby, Chris, for putting up with all those hours of writing, typing, and reading. I love you all!

Thank you, Katie, for forcing me to read that first YA fiction. You started this whole mess!

Thank you, Bub, for being my creative sound board. You'll always be my sci-fi movie buddy.

Thank you, Kim, for getting the chills when I told you I was writing a book. I owe you one, cwesant!

I want to give a very special thank you to my team at Booktrope. Thank you, Samantha March, for organizing my first blog tour, for being a great mentor, and for being my book manager. Thank you, Jesse James Freeman, for taking a chance on me. Thank you, Cathy Shaw, for editing and proofing my novels, and thank you, Greg Simanson, for my covers.